A NAUGHTY LESSON

A STUDY HARD ROMANCE

MIKA LANE

HEADLANDS PUBLISHING

COPYRIGHT

Copyright© 2022 by Mika Lane
Headlands Publishing
4200 Park Blvd. #244
Oakland, CA 94602

ISBN ebook 978-1-948369-80-0
ISBN print 978-1-948369-81-7

BE THE FIRST TO KNOW...

Want more heat, heart,
and bad boys who know what they're doing?
Join my list and I'll send the steam straight to your inbox,
starting with a deliciously naughty story:

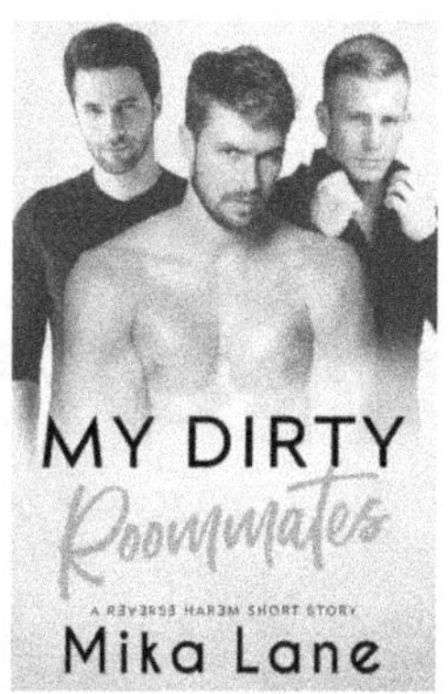

SIGN UP TO MY MAILING LIST!
Or visit:
https://geni.us/free-book-signup

1

BIRDIE JOHNSON

It was true.

People really *did* have sex in libraries.

Couldn't they just wait to get back to their dorm rooms?

What if they got something on the books? Or the tables? Or the chairs?

Or the walls?

I slowed my cart—not slow enough to appear as if I cared, but slow enough to get an earful— and pretended to reshelve the books piled on it.

And an earful, I got. Holy shit.

But I figured, if you're going to have sex in a campus library, the reference floor—where I was working that day—was probably as good a place as any, if not better. With every college student's ability to do so much research online these days, the reference floor was becoming a sad relic of the past, smelling of dusty old books no longer lovingly paged through in the quest for scholarly advancement. I seldom visited it, there were so few books that needed reshelving there, but when I did, it was like entering a morgue. Cold, airless, dark, and dead silent.

That was, unless someone had taken the opportunity to seize on the privacy of the place and play hide the sausage. Or whatever they were doing.

Somebody—or *somebodies*—were getting it on out of sight, down at the end of a towering row of bookshelves, one you probably wouldn't wander down unless you were looking for something highly specialized, or had a thing for the creepy, poorly-lit stacks of the campus library.

Or were looking for a spot to get laid.

The funny thing was, that while the imposing and mostly-deserted room was creepily quiet aside from the occasional laptop keyboard click, slow turn of a page, or a dust-induced cough, the not-so-discreet coeds having the time of their lives were completely unconcerned that their joyful exuberance and screams of passion slammed off the walls, only partly absorbed by the tons of paper surrounding them.

When they paused for breath, someone on the other side of the room giggled.

Instead of being concerned about the racket they were creating, they seemed more focused on how quickly they could get off. Guess I couldn't blame them. They needed to finish their dirty deed and get the hell out before they were caught by someone who gave a damn about what went on in the reference stacks.

I glanced down the nearest aisle then in front of and behind me, to make sure I wasn't being watched by the few now-amused folks trying to study, and inched a little closer to the amorous couple, the fingers of my right hand twisting and tugging on my hair like I always did when I was nervous.

"Oh! Oh! Oh fuck! Harder, harder, yes!" a female voice panted.

A small wave of guilt washed over me, as if I were some perverted voyeur. But on the other hand, it wasn't as if the lovebirds were concerned about privacy. It was as if they wanted to be caught.

Maybe that was the point.

I'd heard having sex in public places was a thing. That some people were really into it, getting a huge rush out of the risk of being caught. I guess those were the people who had sex in airplanes, public restrooms, and elevators.

Which was so not my thing. Not that I *had* a thing, per se.

Personally, I didn't have sex in public places. Nor did I have sex in non-public places.

I actually didn't have sex anywhere.

Because I'd never had sex.

True story.

But I wasn't above listening to people who *were*.

My ears pricked at the sound of the guy grunting, almost growling, really. That, coupled with the female's moans and whimpers, went straight to my—well, let's just say I'd have something to think about later that night when I was in bed, ready to fall asleep, pleasuring myself like I did most every night.

I might have been a virgin, but I wasn't an idiot. I knew how shit worked. Well, at least how my shit worked.

Their enthusiasm reached a crescendo that I thought might bring campus security running. I didn't want to be there when that happened. So, I scurried away deeper into an opposite row of bookshelves to put away the last of the volumes on my cart. I needed to get the hell out of there before someone of authority happened by and wondered why I, as a part-time employee of the campus library, didn't alert the powers that be that inappropriate behavior was taking place in the reference room.

The poor, neglected, reference room. Like a once-beautiful ship past its prime, it was rusty and leaking and unwanted.

But I wasn't ready to bolt just yet. I positioned myself, half-hidden, where I'd have a view of the lovers when they finally exited the stacks. I wanted to see who they were. Yeah, I was a nosy bitch.

And just as I dragged out the shelving of my last book—a dreadful compendium of local nineteenth century tax records and census information—I heard soft tittering.

Yes!

They were leaving. Perfect timing.

A moment later, the girl came out first, one I vaguely recognized—a tall, skinny blonde with a pink streak in her hair, in a *Wellshire University* hoodie and yoga pants. No surprise there—she looked like every other pretty girl on campus. No, what got me was when I realized she was followed by not one guy... but *two*. A burly dude with shaggy brown hair wearing jeans and a tight blue t-shirt, and a lean, athletic guy wearing basketball shorts and a New York Knicks shirt. Did I know him? Maybe from freshman English? James was possibly his name?

'Course, he had no idea of mine.

It didn't matter though, because I'd just heard a real *ménage a trois*.

I knew of such encounters. But they were kind of like advanced-level sex. Top shelf stuff. And while I wouldn't have minded a threesome of my own, I had to first work my way off the bottom-most shelf, where I was stuffed in the back, out of sight and forgotten. There were mountains to climb before I could hope for anything so fancy.

But a girl could dream.

The *trois* were chatting and laughing on their way out, and the 'maybe' James noticed me staring. He smiled and winked, putting a finger to his perfect, still-moist lips.

I quickly looked away, heat washing over my embarrassed face. I had so many questions.

Sex with *two* guys? How does that even work? And beyond that, how was such a thing even arranged?

Was one of them her boyfriend and the other his friend?

Or were the guys together and they invited the girl for a walk on the wild side?

Lucky bitch. I didn't know what sex with *one* guy was like, much less two.

Not for lack of trying, or interest, at least on my part. It just hadn't happened yet.

And I wasn't sure how to make it happen. I mean, was it the kind of thing where someone just walked up to you on the way to class one day, all casual, saying, "Hi, I'm Matt. We're in chemistry together. Wanna have sex?"

I'd been in line at the dining hall a few days earlier and overheard a guy on his cell. "Bro, you have to come up and visit some weekend. Seriously, you just fall into pussy here. It's almost like you can't avoid it."

What?

Really?

How was this part of college life passing me by?

I took a despondent, deep breath, inhaling more of the reference room dustiness than I should have, and waited until I was sure the girl and two guys were gone. I approached the end of the stack where they'd been carrying on, slowly, unsure of what I might find there. One of the duties of all library employees, no matter where you were in the hierarchy, was to make sure the place remained spotless. No coffee cups or stray books were to be left behind.

No condoms or bodily fluids, either, I imagined. Although they'd never been specifically mentioned.

But I was pleased to see the happy little group had left no trace of their deed. There was not only no sign that they'd messed around, I couldn't even tell anyone had been in the vicinity.

These guys were pros.

Satisfied, I headed for the elevator to get back to the main library floor, painfully sensitized to the couples and groups around me, with their little touches indicating familiarity and affection—hugs, kisses, hellos, goodbyes, footsies under the tables, the occasional lob of a balled-up piece of paper—all indications of connections being made that might lead to sex.

Every Wellshire student seemed to have found his or her match—or matches.

Everyone except me.

When I'd dumped the cart and returned to the check-out desk, my co-worker Angelo grabbed me by the arm so hard it hurt. "Birdie, you won't believe the shit I just saw," he hissed.

Ha. For once, I had a story of my own. Angelo was going to be proud. And I was willing to bet it topped anything he had seen. But to be nice, I raised my eyebrows and invited him to continue.

"Right when I got here, when I'd just clocked in," he said breathlessly, "I found two guys on the first floor making out. Like, hot and heavy, you know? Right in the poetry aisle. The boss saw them, too."

Oops.

Our boss, who'd been at the school since before most of us current students were even born, was easily shocked, and I could only imagine what such a sighting might do to her. On the other hand, it was funny to think that someone could spend so much time around horny college undergrads and still be a prude.

"Oh my god," I said. "And in the poetry section!"

"Exactly." Angelo laughed. "So. Hot. I wanted to join them so bad. They were super-cute."

The boss considered poetry sacred. She would not have thought it hot.

"Anyway, thanks again for covering for me earlier," he added.

"Sure. Anytime. Hope you got your paper done."

It wasn't like my calendar was bursting with stuff to do anyway, aside from exam dates and crap like that.

But Angelo—like everyone else around me—was having lots of sex, which only solidified what had become my opinion about the social scene at Wellshire U.

If you were a guy?

Sex.

If you were a girl in a sorority?

Sex.

If you were a girl with big boobs?

Sex.

If you were a girl with blonde hair?

Sex.

If you were a nerdy girl with curly brown hair?

No sex for you!

College had been great for me on an academic level. I'd hit the dean's list three semesters running. I enjoyed working at the library, and I adored my roommate Jessa and her BFF Roxy. But there was something missing from my life, even beyond wanting a hand to hold or mouth to kiss or a guy to Netflix and chill with.

I still had an ache deep inside that desperately needed to be scratched.

Preferably by a hard dick.

I had a paper due at the end of the week, so once I clocked out of work, I went and found a secluded corner of the library where I couldn't see anyone doing the mating dance. I fired up my laptop, and got to work. I was cranking, getting my shit done. Despite the lack of romance in my life, I was feeling pretty good.

Only problem was that I'd been so immersed in my writing I'd lost complete track of time. Despite hustling across campus, the dining hall doors were locked when I arrived.

Dinner was over.

Shit.

I trudged back to the dorm and hit the vending machine in the lobby for a Coke, bag of chips, and a Butterfinger. Disgusting, yes, but it would get me through until morning, when I planned to be first in line for dining hall eggs and bacon.

Passing the common area, I noticed one of the girls who lived down the hall from me and a football player dry humping on the ratty couch by the ping pong table.

Which just proved my point. Why go all the way to the library when you can just have sex in the dorm rec room?

I dragged myself up the stairs to the third floor, where I shared a room with Jessa. But before I reached my door, the one next to us was bursting with the sounds we had all learned to expect from the woman who lived there. She had a single, meaning no room-mate. That meant more privacy, and *that* meant more fun.

Her noisiness had started out as annoying, but the entire floor had come to see it as comical. My neighbor had frequent, and obnoxiously performative sex. To the uninitiated, her screams and shrieks might sound as if she were being murdered, but as it turned out she had just watched way too much porn, and her way of showing her date—and everybody else in the dorm— that she was enjoying herself was to mimic a baboon warning his troops of danger.

I chuckled as I passed, and just before slipping my key in my lock, the girl from across the hall arrived with a guy in tow. She smiled and gave me a little wave. He nodded. "Sup?" he asked without making eye contact—a sure sign they were not available for small talk.

No, they had business to attend to.

I mumbled a hello and leaned into my door. *How the fuck many Wellshire students were hooking up today? All of them, save one?*

Apparently.

Safely ensconced in my room, I burrowed into my junk food, happy that out of the view of prying eyes, I wasn't reminding anyone I was the only person on the Wellshire campus not getting any nooky.

I ate slowly, a bite of my Butterfinger away from finishing, when there was a key in my door. Jessa came bouncing into the room with Roxy, a regular visitor, in tow.

The smell hit me before I even saw anything, and my heart leapt for joy.

"We thought you might be hungry, so we smuggled you out a slice." Roxy produced a paper plate from under her jacket-draped arm—a large, floppy slice of dining hall pizza under a grease-spotted napkin.

While our dining hall pizza could be described as 'tomato sauce spread over cardboard and doused with enough grease to change the oil in a car,' at the moment it smelled and looked delicious, and I didn't care how it might taste. I hungrily accepted.

"Sounds like somebody is having fun next door," Roxy giggled, gesturing over her shoulder with a thumb.

"She's been going for a good twenty minutes with no break," I said.

"Either her guy fucks like a stallion or she's trying to win an Oscar," Jessa said.

Maybe both.

"Have you seen him?" I asked. "He's no stallion."

Unless scrawny and a sour expression were your thing.

When I finished my slice, we chatted about school, and I told them how proud I was of myself that I'd nearly finished my paper. But then it occurred to me why I had surpassed my goals so easily.

"Oh no," I whined, and slapped my bed with both hands, startling everyone. "I got so wrapped up in that assignment I completely forgot the creative writing one I have due tomorrow. Fuck!"

"What's it about?" Roxy asked.

I scrolled through the calendar on my phone. "The whole thing just slipped my mind. Ugh, the last thing I want to do tonight is more writing. Okay, here it is."

I found it in the class notes I'd emailed myself. "*Tell us about something that comes easily for others but not for you.* That's the premise. Just a thousand words. But still."

"Have the sex queen do it," Jessa suggested, cringing as our neighbor's passion shook our shared wall.

Between her nights of theatrical fucking, she was actually a pretty good writer who did papers for money—any topic, any length. Regardless of being highly against every rule of Wellshire University, word had it she made enough to pay her tuition and then some.

And a thousand words would be easy for her, practically guaranteeing an A.

The problem was I was close to broke, and she didn't work for free.

Not that I'd let anyone do my work for me, anyway. I was perfectly capable of earning my own A, something Jessa and Roxy like to remind me of.

"Nah. I'd never do that. Nor could I afford it, anyway," I said.

My last paycheck from the library had been spent on books. There was nothing left. Not a single cent.

"I don't know what you'd write about, anyway" Roxy said. "You're smart, you get good grades, you're super cute, your parents are not only together, but they help pay for some of your school—unlike *mine*. So, what's a challenge for Birdie Johnson?"

I opened my mouth to answer, but Jessa cut me off.

"She can't make it to the dining hall in time because she's in the library studying so long. Poor Birdie!"

We laughed.

"I know, right, Jessa? What a burden, getting all those A's," Roxy teased. "But seriously. Is there anybody at Wellshire having an easier time than you, Birdie? After I scrape together my tuition every semester, my next worry is 'Can I bump a C to barely-a-B if I put in a bunch of extra time studying?' Yours is 'How much extra studying will it take to turn my default A into an A+?'"

I shrugged. She wasn't wrong. Not that the academic side of college was exactly *easy*, but I watched some of my friends and classmates scratch and claw and work themselves into stress-related anxiety attacks to get a two-point zero GPA, and I had a tough time relating. Maybe I just knew how to study better or had learned a more efficient path from lecture and textbook to brain? Who knew? What I *did* know was that there was indeed one aspect of college life that had proven to be an insurmountable challenge for me.

"I'm the only virgin on campus, so there's that," I blurted out, and it suddenly felt like all the air was sucked out of the room.

"For real?" Roxy whispered when she recovered.

Jessa knew my secret and patted me on the back. As if that would make me feel better.

"Yep," I added. "The whole school is having sex, some constantly." I motioned in the direction of my neighbor's room. "But not *moi*," I said, pointing at myself with my thumb.

"Maybe sex queen is trying to build up a rep as a porn star for when she finally gets caught and expelled for writing people's term papers. Besides, Birdie, there are plenty of people on campus who aren't having sex," Jessa said.

"There were three people fucking in the stacks of the reference room today. A *ménage a trois*. It's all around us, Jessa, I'm telling you," I said flatly. "It's everybody, everywhere."

Their eyes grew wide, and I shared the reference room story after making them beg for a minute or two.

"Well then," Roxy said hopefully, "you ought to just write about that."

Jessa shrugged. "Why not? It'll be well-written, and that's what matters way more than the content. Only the professor is going to see it anyway, so who cares?"

It was a thought. But not one I was wild about. Professor Blake was smart and funny and so handsome in that twinkle-eyed, square-jawed George Clooney sort of way that I practically melted every time he walked into the classroom. But so did all the other females in class, as well as a few males. Seriously. You'd never seen a class of college students hang on a teacher's every word quite the way they did Professor Blake's.

And he probably thought they were enthralled with his brilliant teaching.

Not to take anything away from him. But no one was that good.

Earlier in the day, I'd spotted him in the library. But did I hold my head up, push my shoulders back, and approach him for a friendly little chat?

Hell no.

I couldn't handle that man in a one-on-one away from the classroom. Or even *in* the classroom. No, I had no desire for a conversation with him at any time, about anything.

All I needed was to turn into a useless puddle of mush at my library job, and my boss would be all over my ass.

So, best to avoid him altogether.

"I saw a Reddit post where these dudes claim that if they don't masturbate, they get superpowers," Jessa said, interrupting my reverie. "Or maybe it was if they didn't have orgasms. I can't remember. Like it would make them smarter and stronger. I always thought, 'No, dumbass, it's because instead of whacking off all the time, you're going to the gym or hitting the books or doing something else productive, so at the end of the day you've accomplished something.'"

Roxy laughed, and I gave a half-hearted chuckle.

"Maybe so," I said quietly, my shoulders slumping.

"Oh, B, it was just a joke," Jessa said. "My point is that getting laid is not the answer to everything. Maybe that's why you do so well in school. You're not wasting your *chi*."

"Perhaps. But the whole thing has been bugging me lately for some reason," I said.

"Then you should definitely write about it," Roxy insisted. "To help you process it, you know? And we can even proofread it for you or help you edit it. Okay?"

"Sure. Why not," I said, pulling out my laptop.

I didn't exactly want Professor Hottie knowing my deep, dark secrets, but on the other hand, who cared? The semester would eventually end and I'd never see him again, anyway. I had only a few hours to pull this assignment together, and now was not the time to fret about my pride.

I'd have plenty of time for that later.

21

2

PROFESSOR CARY BLAKE

IT HAD BEEN a long-running struggle with the barista to get my coffee order right. There were only so many possible variations, and she had mastered them all. But for some reason I received the actual coffee I ordered every morning only once every ten days or so. It was like a rotation. *Guess what coffee I'm giving you today? Not the one you ordered!*

There were bigger problems in the world, though, and while I could be a dick and scream about it, I didn't want to be *that guy.*

So, I chalked it up to the coffee gods hating me for whatever transgressions I'd committed in a past life. On that particular morning, however, the wayward barista had added just the right amount of foam, sweetener, and coffee to my beverage, shocking me into silence. I smiled at her as I left, and on my trek across campus, I found myself looking forward to the day. A professor from the history department high-fived me as he jogged in the opposite direction, and a former student, a favorite of mine, slowed down to ask if I needed a ride. I thanked him for the offer, but the weather was too spectacular to sit in a car, especially given that I'd be cooped up in a classroom or office for the rest of the day.

It was funny how the little things could make your day.

Actually, things were going my way for reasons more important than a well-made coffee drink and seeing a few people I liked. I had a top-notch TA, my students were mostly able to compose grammatically correct—if uninspired—paragraphs in the English language, and best of all, my soon-to-be-ex was, well, soon to be my ex.

Which was a long goddamn time coming.

My happy balloon was violently popped, however, the moment I got to my office.

Sitting on one of the chairs outside my door was none other than Joan. Joan Judge.

The soon-to-be-ex.

I stopped short, pretending to be confused by my surroundings. "Hello, Joan. Didn't realize I was in the psych building. Must have taken a wrong turn somewhere on campus."

My ex was a brilliant professor of psychology. I had to give her that. And there was a time, not so very long ago, that I'd have done anything to ensure our paths crossed, including taking all the wrong turns on campus I needed to. I'd thought of her day and night, even after I'd convinced her to marry me.

But now, not so much. Things had gone rotten, like a carton of spoiled milk. The kind that sneaks up on you until *bam*, you realize your life is nothing but curdled stinkiness.

And now that our marriage had disintegrated, it was a small mercy that the psychology and English departments were separated by a large chunk of the Wellshire campus.

Thus the reason her showing up outside my office was a surprise. And not a pleasant one.

"Good morning, Cary," she said dryly. "It seems that ambushing you is the only way to track you down. It was either here or at your little love shack, but I couldn't bear the thought of watching some poor coed endure the walk of shame while her professor watches her sad exit through his front window."

No fucking way. This again? She was still on my ass with her paranoid suspicions about my supposed trysts with my students.

Trysts that had never, ever occurred. In spite of having had every opportunity, I'd only wanted her since the day I laid eyes on her.

But, in her mind, they *had* happened.

How do you argue with a mind that refuses to be changed?

And as I absorbed the daggers shooting at me from her eyes, I realized I was tired. Tired of her accusations, tired of her hate, and tired of her paranoia, which had brought about the end of our marriage.

"Maybe I should have made an appointment?" she taunted.

When the Wellshire University student body decided to do nominations for RateMyProf.com a year before, for some reason I'd scored highly. In fact, I'd come in second out of all the school's male professors. Number one had been a visiting Argentine guest lecturer who resembled Antonio Banderas. When Joan saw the results, instead of being happy that her husband was considered desirable in a silly little contest, she went ballistic and ramped up the cheating accusations.

Furthermore, she had reversed course on something we'd agreed on before ever getting married, which was whether or not to have children. I hadn't planned on it, was strongly opposed, and never wavered. She'd always been enthusiastic in her agreement, happy for the freedom to focus on her career and our cozy little marriage. But when things started getting wobbly, she reversed course and was convinced having a baby would cure the schism between us.

Terrible idea, I insisted, to introduce such stress to an already unstable relationship, but she wouldn't let the idea drop. Eventually attorneys were retained, and divorce papers were drawn up.

Sadly, and needlessly, the split was less than amicable. With no custody issues to resolve and few assets to divide, I'd hoped and expected that it might be peaceful. Evidently, Joan had other ideas.

"How are we supposed to petition the court to grant the divorce when we still have so much unsettled business?" she snapped, following me into my office.

I set my coffee down and took a seat behind my desk.

She stood, hand on hip, glaring at me as I powered up my laptop and logged into email as if she might decide to leave me alone so I could start my day in peace.

Yeah, right.

After a long drink from my cup, I leaned back in my chair and put my hands behind my head.

"What *unsettled* business, Joan?" I asked. "We have no children. No house. I'm getting direct deposit into my bank account, you into yours. I've signed over the car to you, hell, I've even said you can keep the bloody plants. You have the house and I've moved out and taken my clothes and personal effects. What else is there to discuss?"

The only sticking point was Wilbur, our pug, but we'd agreed to a joint custody arrangement, as we both loved that adorable dog and no matter how much animosity existed between us, we didn't want him to suffer. He'd go back and forth between our homes as long as it was logistically feasible.

She made an awful 'Harrumph!' sound and continued glaring. I shrugged and scrolled through my email, searching for anything interesting.

"You're just *so* pleased with yourself, aren't you?" Joan said. "You have it *all* figured out."

I sighed and looked at the ceiling and the fluorescent lamp flickering overhead. "I already said I'll come over this weekend to get my books. Honestly, you can keep everything else. If you find something of mine that you don't want, throw it away, give it away, sell it, I don't care. I really don't. Now if you'll excuse me, I have class to prepare for." I looked at my watch. "I imagine you do, too, and yours is all the way across campus."

"*Now* you've suddenly become concerned about my *whens* and *wheres*?" she sneered.

Jesus. She was really jonesing for a conflict. And she was going to keep jonesing, because she wasn't going to have one with me.

I forced a smile. "I'll see you this weekend for my books," I said, brushing past.

"Asshole," she hissed as I headed out, hoping like hell she'd be gone when I got back from class.

I cleared my throat loudly as I entered the classroom, and my students came to some semblance of order.

I scanned the room for attendance and wasn't surprised to find the back-left corner—allegedly home to a cluster of football players—completely vacant.

The front row featured the usual suspects, a collection of sorority girls smiling flirtatiously, trying to catch my eye by crossing and uncrossing their legs, barely covered by the short skirts they wore.

Front and center was the prettiest of them all, a solid C student whose blonde hair had a pink streak in it, also wearing a skirt so short I questioned its legality. She sat back and lewdly spread her legs, evidently to shock or seduce, and shimmied forward in her seat so I had a clear view of her black, lacy panties.

I rolled my eyes, shook my head, and sighed. The campus was filled with guys—I hesitate to call most of them *men*, but that's an opinion informed by a perspective of age that they lack—who had to be all kinds of horny, if my memory of college was accurate. Why come after *me* so aggressively?

I didn't get the appeal. I just didn't.

"Okay, people," I said. "I'll come around and collect the 'Something that comes easily for others, but not for you' essays. Everyone who deigned to show up, that is." I waved my hand toward the football corner, eliciting a laugh.

As I walked to the far side of the room amid a shuffling of papers, a hand in the second row shot up.

"Professor Blake?" A exceedingly average student who crammed Quentin Tarantino references into everything he wrote and whose mission in life seemed to be to annoy me at every turn, called my name. "You said that wasn't due until next week."

Snickers filled the room.

"I did?" I asked, surprised. "Remind me."

"The other day," he sputtered. "Last week or I can't exactly remember, but for sure you did. One hundred percent. You said you had to delay it since you wouldn't have time to grade them because of… I don't remember, you had to go to the foot doctor or something."

"Oh, that's right," I said, playing along. "I have a marathon appointment with my podiatrist that's expected to last at least four days. Thank you for reminding me. No time at all to grade papers." Little did they know, even if I did have such an appointment, my teaching assistant would be handling the bulk of the work anyway. The class laughed, and it was Tyler's turn to look annoyed.

"Does anyone concur with Tyler?" I asked the class. "Does anyone share this memory of his?"

"Dumbass," a guy in the back row muttered, and he was showered with a chorus of cheers. As I looked around, to my surprise, it seemed every other student had papers in hand ready to give to me.

"It seems you may be confused, my friend," I said. "But I'm feeling charitable. If you have your paper to me first thing in the morning, with no reference to your hero, Quentin Tarantino, I'll accept it as on- time. But the rest of you—don't get any ideas," I continued. "This is a one-time deal for my star student, Tyler."

There were a few laughs and more than a few groans from students who were evidently aggrieved by Tyler's 'special treatment,' so I decided to win the group back over.

I was still perturbed by Joan's out-of-the-blue appearance, and in not in much of a mood to conduct class anyway.

As I collected the completed essays, I made a surprise announcement.

"Since I can't wait to get started with these," I held up the stack in my hand, "and because it's such a nice day, class is dismissed."

Cheers, smiles, and high-fives followed. As usual, the class cleared out like a mini-stampede, and I returned to my office.

I set aside the papers for my TA and read the two emails Joan had sent in the time it took me to get to class, collect my students' papers, and return to my office.

She was nothing if not efficient.

3

BIRDIE JOHNSON

PROFESSOR HOTTIE HADN'T SEEMED himself, but there wasn't anything I could do about that. I mean, shit, I couldn't even handle a conversation with the man. So, I handed him my paper, enjoyed his fresh, clean scent, and hummed to myself as I returned to the dorm.

Getting out of class early was always a nice surprise, but this time my happiness was short-lived.

"Hey. You're back early," Jessa said as I walked in. She was lying on her bed, facing away from me, reading something I couldn't see.

Probably something from one of her the art magazines she subscribed to in preparation for her career as the next Picasso.

"Class let out early after we handed in our papers," I said. "Got that sucker out of the way, thanks to you and Roxy."

I was scrolling through my online calendar to get a

33

look at the rest of the week when Jessa bolted up on her bed, staring at me, wide-eyed.

"Something wrong?" I asked.

She was pale.

"Well, um, Birdie—Roxy and I were kind of kidding about your essay topic. You know, the one about your… *virginity*," she said in a high-pitched voice.

She thrust a copy of my English essay at me.

She hadn't been reading one of her art magazines.

"Where'd you get this?"

"You left it in the printer. I guess you accidentally printed two copies. I wasn't going to read it until I figured out it was… you know…"

I shrugged. "Oh. That's okay. I don't mind your reading it."

But why was she giving it back to me like it smelled bad or something?

Her mouth opened, then closed, and she looked at me with a blank stare.

What the hell?

"Jessa? What?" I asked. "Why do you look like someone died?"

"We… we were *joking* yesterday. About your paper. You weren't really supposed to do it. You know? Weren't you just playing along? You weren't really supposed to write about your… sex life. Or lack thereof."

Huh?

"Wh… what do you mean? I… I thought it was a good idea. You guys… gave me the idea."

Jessa looked at me like I was a complete dumbass. "Well, what's done is done. I'm sure you'll get an A. And that's all that matters, right?"

Tears stung the corner of my eyes, where my crying always began.

"What part of 'Yeah, Birdie, write about your virginity' was a joke, Jessa? I didn't hear any kidding in your voice. You sounded dead serious. And now you're telling me I made a mistake? It's a little late for that, don't you think?"

I was trying to remain calm, but my voice was becoming more shrill with each word.

"So you… actually turned it in?" she asked.

"Yeah. Of course I did. About fifteen minutes ago. Thanks to *your* encouragement," I snapped, wiping at an unwelcome tear. "What's… what's so bad about my paper? I mean, it's the truth."

I attempted a strangled laugh.

How bad could it be?

Jessa thought for a moment. "You know, I think there's still time to drop that class," she said. "You surely can't show your face there again. Personally, I would be *mortified.*"

I wanted to kill her. Or at least cause her a good deal of pain.

"First, Jessa, thanks for setting me up to make a fool of myself—"

She waved her hands wildly. "I didn't. I didn't mean for you to actually write it—" she interrupted.

But I cut her off. "And thanks for saying my problem is… *mortifying,* to use your term."

With friends like this…

Her eyes widened as she started to back pedal. "Whoa, Birdie, slow down. It isn't *that* serious," she said lightly.

She threw in a chuckle for good measure.

But it was too late. I gathered my things in a huff and split, slamming the door behind me. I had a little extra time before I was due for my library shift, but I wasn't going to spend it looking at someone I was itching to strangle.

Much too tempting.

My phone buzzed as I marched across campus, text messages from both Jessa and Roxy pouring in like scrolling credits at the end of a movie. But I wasn't ready to deal with them, my so-called friends, so as I cut across campus with my head down, I almost crashed into somebody equally unaware of his surroundings.

I managed to avoid a major body-to-body collision, but in sidestepping each other, I still somehow managed to tussle with the casualty of my inattention. The guy dropped the big, hard-back book he'd been reading while walking, as well as a large stack of papers he'd had stuffed under one arm.

"Oh, sorry, so sorry," he muttered, bending to retrieve his things which, thanks to a small breeze, were starting to flutter away.

"Here. Let me help you," I said, springing into action.

I grabbed everything I could within my reach, and when I had the papers in a jumbled pile, I took off after the one blowing across the grass.

"Holy crap, what a mess," he said, taking the crumpled papers from my hands. "Thank you so much. I knew I should have put these in a folder or something."

As I caught my breath, I finally took a good look at him, and realized I knew him.

"You're Professor Blake's TA, right?" I asked.

He looked at me, surprised. "Yeah. I'm Kai. Kai Fleminster."

Like I didn't already know that.

The guy was hard to forget. First, he gave Professor Hottie a run for his money in the looks department. Second, he always wore flip flops, no matter the weather, pairing them with ratty jeans and a half-tucked-in yellow and black flannel shirt. He was a borderline mess, but an adorable one. Ginger-haired absent-minded professor meets Prince Harry, with a week's growth of red scruff on his face.

He'd come by our class a few times, I guessed to hear Professor Blake's lecture. The class didn't know what to make of him and his sloppy attire as compared to the professor's, which was pretty immaculate.

They were a funny pair, I remember thinking.

"Thanks for your help. I appreciate it," he said, still trying to get organized.

Shit. Was he carrying the papers my class had just turned in?

"Um, Kai, do you have a sec for a question? About Professor Blake's English class? You work with him, right?"

He nodded. "Yeah. I support him and Professor Vale. What's your question? And what did you say your name was?"

Cripes, he was smiling at me now, and I knew I was moments away from losing my words and melting into an incoherent idiot.

So I spoke fast.

"My name is Birdie. Birdie Johnson. And Kai, you may know that in Professor Blake's class today we had an essay due. After some thought, I decided I hate mine. I'm sure I can do much better, and I'd like to switch mine out. I could do a rewrite super-fast and get it to the two of you tomorrow. He gave somebody else in our class an extension, so I was thinking, you could give me back the paper I handed in and I'll get cracking on the replacement."

I smiled hopefully. If I had been one of the campus pretty girls, that's when I would have tossed my blonde hair back and stuck my chest out.

But I had a feeling this guy might be oblivious to that sort of thing, anyway.

He scrunched his fingers through his facial scruff. "I'm afraid not, Billie, because—"

"Birdie," I interrupted.

"Birdie, that's right," he said, nodding, his red hair

ruffling in the breeze. "Problem is, once a paper has been submitted, it's impossible to exchange it. It's a crazy university rule. I don't know where it came from, but I know I have to enforce it. Sorry 'bout that."

He turned to go, leaving me standing there on the sidewalk, deflated and horrified that I was stupid enough to share my biggest personal problem with a professor and his assistant who were, pretty much, strangers to me.

I watched Kai open his book back up to read while he was walking, the class papers, including my especially sensitive story, barely held in place by his underarm. He was on his way somewhere, for sure—to ruin my life.

I could always kick him in the shin, grab the papers, and run.

Or not.

Fact was, my fate was sealed. Soon, Professor Blake, his teaching assistant, the English department, my class, and eventually the whole fucking school would know I was the only student on campus who wasn't getting laid, and who had never even gotten laid.

4

KAI FLEMINSTER

I KNEW I shouldn't read while walking.

But the fact was, I'd been doing it all my life. Most everywhere I went, I had a book open. I'd gotten pretty good at keeping my eyes on the page, and my peripheral vision on my surroundings.

But my aim wasn't perfect, so to speak. At least I hadn't run into the dean or someone else who might one day be a decision-maker when it came to my career as a professor at Wellshire University. But even if I had run into some university bigwig, I had an ace up my sleeve. I'd be the third generation of Fleminsters to teach at Wellshire, a family tradition started by my grandfather, followed by my own father, and now under pursuit by me.

It would be an honor to follow in the footsteps of them, both distinguished in their service to the university. And while it might be a leg up that they paved the way for me, it was far from a done deal.

But, thankfully, I'd only run into one of Professor Cary Blake's and my English students, and a very pretty one at that. Poor thing practically begged for her essay back, but I couldn't do a thing to help her.

And now I found myself rushing to Cary's office, where we were to have our weekly meeting. But when I arrived, I found him with his officemate Professor Leo Vale talking and laughing, unbothered one bit by my tardiness.

Cary waved me into the office and turned back to Leo, slapping his thigh. "I'm telling you, she just isn't my type, Leo, even if I were looking to 'hook up' or whatever."

I squeezed behind his chair and set my things down on my small desk in the corner of the already-small office.

"Oh, please, that girl is *everybody's* type," Leo insisted, rolling his eyes. "And you're newly single. You know, if you need some help, I'm sure somebody over in the med school has samples of something that will put the lead back in your pencil, if that's the problem."

I never minded playing fly-on-the-wall while Leo and Cary bantered back and forth. They were smart and funny as hell, and I couldn't have asked for better mentors.

Cary snorted. "Old man, I'll outrun, out-teach, out-write, and out-fuck you any day of the week and twice on Sunday, no little blue pill required, thank you very much."

This sent Leo into peals of laughter.

"Kai, you should have been here five minutes ago," he said, catching his breath from laughing so hard. "One of Cary's students just came in here—a nine-point-five if not a perfect ten—and practically threw herself at him, with me sitting right here. I thought one of them might be turning to me to ask for a freaking condom, that's how hot they were getting."

Cary held his hands up like a *stop* sign. "Hey now, there was nothing heating up in this room aside from your sick imagination, my friend. I straightened that coed right out. She won't be back here."

Leo smacked his hand on his forehead. "You know what? I'm pretty sure she has Darlington for econ. Think she's headed over there right now to *discuss* her grade? I'm not sure he'll turn her away as readily as you did."

Oh shit. I'd heard the campus scuttlebutt about Darlington. The man was not a model of discretion.

Leo stood up and bent over Cary's desk, abandoning his normal baritone for a squeaky falsetto, and sashaying his hips. "Professor Blake, I just don't know if I can pass your class. It's so *haaaard.* I think I might need some one-on-one attention." Leo sauntered two steps across our office, which was really as far as you could go in the tight space, laughing.

"Who was the student?" I asked, dying to know.

"She sits in the front row of my ten o'clock class," Cary said. "Showed off her panties today. Seems to have trouble keeping her knees together. Blonde hair, pretty."

Sounded like half the female students at Wellshire. Maybe even more than half.

My father and grandfather had warned me about 'friendly' students, especially those who offered to do 'whatever it took' to pass or to earn an A.

Only twenty minutes earlier, I'd been chatting with Birdie, and I had to say that under different circumstances, I would have asked her out for coffee. While the blonde student kind of hot was commonplace on a college campus, Birdie's was interesting and rare. Not that I would act on it.

Leo backhanded me on the shoulder. "Yo, Fleminster. You still with us?"

Lost in thought. Again. My fatal flaw.

"Just like his old man," Cary said to his colleague, pointing his thumb toward me. "Your father, Kai, had the attention span of a goldfish. Every seven or eight seconds, the world was brand new to him. Great teacher and man. Conversationalist? Not so much. At least that's how he was when I was *his* TA. He was a good man, Kai."

I laughed. He had my father pegged. Over the span of ten minutes, he could go off on a thousand tangents. He was never boring.

And here I was, ten years later, working with the man who'd worked for my father. It was clear we both missed him.

"Hey Kai, I was saying that we're headed to the gym later. Do you want to join us?" he asked.

"Yeah. Sure. I'm in," I said.

Few of the other TAs who I knew worked with professors as cool as Cary and Leo. Some were little more than glorified personal servants—gofers, sent to fetch coffee and make copies and never spoken to as if they had any possible future in the academic world.

Cary and Leo were different, however, often treating me like an equal, asking me questions and offering more and more responsibility as the year passed. I was one of the lucky ones.

He spotted the pile of essays I'd set down on the corner of my desk.

"Cripes, Kai, what happened to those papers? You drag them through the mud?" he asked. "Are those the ones from my ten o'clock class?"

I nodded, scooping them up and organizing them as best I could. "Yeah. I dropped them on my way here. Hey, did you read any before you gave them to me?"

I wanted to hear his insights before I started babbling about my own. Another important lesson my father and grandfather had taught me about academic life was to be careful with my words at all times. My dad always said there was nothing as political as an academic department at a university.

"I read the first three. I wanted to burn the rest," he sighed.

"Well, I got through a few of them over lunch," I said. They were pretty rough, he was right. "But there's one in particular I really want to read. Like right away."

Cary and Leo watched as I leafed through the messy stack, looking for a paper by one Birdie Johnson. "I ran into a girl from your class on the way over here, and she practically begged to have her essay returned. She'd decided she didn't like it and wanted to do a rewrite. Pretty girl with wild curly hair and beautiful full lips."

"Oh yeah," Cary said. "Would that be Birdie Johnson?"

I nodded as I pulled her paper from the stack.

"She's one of the better writers in that class. Quiet and studious. I saw her in the library yesterday but couldn't manage to catch up with her. What could be in that essay that she wanted to swap out?"

I was wondering the same, and started reading. In an instant, my eyes grew wide.

"Oh shit."

Both professors turned my way.

My face was hot, and beads of sweat gathered on my forehead.

Why did she have to write this essay? Couldn't she have found a dozen other topics?

"Don't keep us in suspense," Leo said.

"Um, Cary, how are these being graded?" I asked when I finished reading.

"We're using the typical grading method. Grammar, style, etcetera," he said impatiently.

"Not content, then," I said. "Okay… it's pretty clear why she wanted her paper back. She wrote about something very… personal. And after having some time to think about it, she probably is sorry she did. Shit, I'd be sorry if I were her, too."

Cripes, I wasn't her and *I* was sorry she'd told her

damn story. How would I ever look her in the eye again?

I passed the paper to Cary. "I think you should read this yourself."

He rolled his head around on his neck like he was relieving tension. "Kai, that is what I have you for. Just give me the highlights."

"Um, well, okay, I said, clearing my throat a couple times. "Birdie's essay is about how she is a… virgin. And that everybody else at Wellshire is having tons of sex. That's her issue, that everyone else gets sex, and she doesn't manage to."

Cary's mouth fell open, and Leo held his hand out. "Give me that paper, Kai. I've got to see it."

He grabbed it from my hands and flipped through the pages, reading at a record speed.

"Holy shit," he mumbled, flipping to the last page. "I've never seen anything like it."

He passed it over to Cary, who was demanding to see it now.

"She's not my student, guys," Leo said, "but I'd sure as hell give her an A."

He looked like he wanted to give her something else, too.

5

BIRDIE JOHNSON

I SPOTTED Professor Blake in the distance, and under any other circumstances I would have veered away, found a place to hide, reversed course, or otherwise avoided him. *Especially* given the fact that it marked the first time I'd seen him since handing in that ridiculous mistake of an essay about being the only virgin on the Wellshire campus.

Mortified didn't begin to describe my state of mind, and it wasn't helped by my fury toward Jessa. Yeah, I'd written the damn essay, but she and Roxy had made me think it was a great idea.

Tell your professor you're a virgin! It will be great!

How stupid was I for listening to them?

So I was in no frame of mind to face Professor Blake just then. The problem was, I was already running a few minutes late for psychology class, and he was standing just outside the building I should have been inside five minutes ago. No way to get inside without passing right by him. Dammit.

And he wasn't just standing there—he was surrounded by three impossibly pretty, perfect, blonde, leggy girls, all clamoring for his attention, giggling at everything he said, batting their eyelashes and doing everything short of removing their clothing to steal his attention.

As I drew nearer, I realized that their presence would actually benefit me, since I could potentially slip inside, unnoticed, while his eyes were stuck on the gaggle of pageant girls in front of him.

My mind wandered to which of them—or all of them—he was hooking up with for an easy A. They were clearly eager, and I didn't imagine many men would turn down girls like that.

I zoned out at the thought of him at the center of some sort of debauched orgy and before I knew it I was almost alongside the group. And because I couldn't help my nosiness, I stole a glance in his direction.

To my horror, he was staring right at me. However briefly, we made eye contact over the heads of his groupies, and I wished that the ground would swallow me up. I imagined all four of them taunting me. *Virgin! Virgin! Freak show!*

That about summed it up.

I turned my head and quickened my pace, taking the steps two at a time and disappearing into the building.

Willing my heart rate to slow down, I stood outside

my psych class room for a minute, hoping I could sneak in without drawing my professor's ire.

Psych had been a general education requirement that I hadn't been too excited about, but it was turning out to be a pretty cool class. The teacher was another story, though. An attractive woman, but cold. Disconnected. *Mean.*

I inched the door open to avoid any squeaking, and slipped into the back of the room, holding very still to avoid attracting any attention. As I lowered myself into the nearest seat, I breathed a sigh of relief over my success.

Not so fast.

Just when I'd opened my notebook, Professor Judge paused her lecture, gave me a disapproving sneer, and continued speaking.

Whatever, lady.

"As I was saying, you should all have signed up for a study by now, and the ones that haven't started yet will in the next couple weeks."

Shit.

As she droned on, I brought up the department web site on my laptop. I'd been meaning to get around to signing up for a study, a stupid requirement of the course. The psych department needed subjects for its research, and clearly looked at the student body as free labor. If we didn't participate, we were automatically given a lower grade.

As much as I was enjoying my psych class, I really couldn't be bothered with being one of the department's guinea pigs. But was it worth getting a B, rather than my usual A?

I thought not.

I followed the links to the signup page, and my heart sank.

Most everything I would have been interested in was already full. There was a lot of availability for locked-in weekend stays at a house off-campus, which sounded like the start of a good horror movie.

No thanks. I had my job, anyway.

Another was a sleep study, but they only wanted people who either snored or talked in their sleep. That eliminated me, not that I wanted to spend the night anywhere other than my own bed.

Because I'd ruled out the first two, I had only one option left.

Human Sexuality.

Oh fuck it. I was out of options. I signed my ass up, wondering what the hell a virgin could possibly contribute to a sexuality research project. If they stuck to masturbation, I was fine. If things got any more involved than that, they were wasting their time.

The study, two weeks out, was added to my calendar. Fantastic. Couldn't wait. I fidgeted through the rest of class, imagining how humiliating the upcoming study would be.

Once class let out, I made sure I was near the center of the exiting herd in case Professor Blake and his entourage were still out front, but of course they weren't. There were classes to attend. And sex to be had.

Regardless of my earlier effort to avoid Professor Blake, I'd been considering stopping by the English Department to clear the air and somehow explain myself. But what the hell would I actually say that my essay hadn't already clearly spelled out?

My story wasn't complicated. It was just pathetic.

I headed toward my dorm, which was in the same general direction as the English department.

Should I? Or shouldn't I?

"Hey, Birdie," a voice behind me called.

Shit. It was the sex queen from next door.

She caught up to me. "Hi. Headed back to the dorm? I'm meeting a new guy there. I'm so excited. He's hung like a—"

"Gotta run, see ya," I said, veering to the right.

In the direction of the English building.

Sometimes decisions were made for you.

I arrived at Professor Blake's door with no idea of what I was going to say. So I just knocked.

The door opened a crack, and I peeked inside. "Professor Blake?"

"No, sorry, he isn't in, is there anything I can do for you?" a voice called back.

Holy shit. Professor Vale.

I had seen Professor Leo Vale around campus a few times, but most often I'd seen his face on a poster of the hottest professors at Wellshire. Right next to Professor Blake's.

How did these guys end up sharing an office? Do they keep the best-looking ones together, away from the common folk, lest their shine fade?

Vale was a published novelist and playwright, not to mention blessed with the most gorgeous of dimples. Once his poster was available, I'd daydreamed about him more than once, and wondered about the lack of a Mrs. Vale in the 'Personal Life' section of his Wikipedia page.

And now, I was face to face with him, where I had his undivided attention. My head was spinning and I was giggly inside.

But I would play it cool.

"Hello. I'm Birdie Johnson, one of Professor Blake's students. Do you know when he'll be back?" I asked breezily.

A small smile spread across Vale's face, and he pulled an empty chair for me. "Hello, Birdie. I think he'll be right back. Would you like to wait here with me until he returns?"

6

PROFESSOR LEO VALE

"IF YOU'RE sure it's no trouble, I'd love to wait," she said, grabbing the offered seat.

Trouble? How much trouble could it be to look at a beautiful young woman who'd just penned an essay about her inability to lose her virginity?

To say I was intrigued was an understatement. To say I was turned on was an understatement, too.

Down boy.

But seriously. What was it about a modest, unassuming woman that was my kryptonite?

I'd always had a thing for the girl next door. And this one fit the bill in spades. She had thick, curly brown hair spilling down her shoulders, framing a beautiful face most remarkable for its pillowy, delicious lips.

She was unique in her normality. I think that's what it was. Nothing about her was forced, from the slightly crooked teeth her smile revealed, to the scuffed-up

Chuck Taylor sneakers she wore with mismatched socks. So many coeds at Wellshire tried so hard to be pretty, sexy, cute, and in every other way attractive. In my view, it came off as desperately forced, from the makeup to the skirts that got shorter and tighter every year, to the Kardashian-inspired vocal fry that was supposed to be sexy and cool.

Birdie Johnson had none of that. There was an authenticity to her, a quiet confidence that she was what she was, take it or leave it, and she wouldn't be troubled either way. Except I knew there *was* something bothering her, which she'd made the topic of the essay she had no idea I'd read.

To be honest, if even one of my classes had a few of her kind sprinkled in among the Stepford students, the notion of leaving academia wouldn't be so appealing.

Leaving academia.

There, I'd said it. Well, I'd not said it out loud. Only in my mind and even then, it pained me terribly. The very thought broke my heart to the point where I couldn't utter the words. I'd not even been able to discuss it with anyone save my officemate, Cary, and even then I was vague about what I had on my mind.

What do you do when something you'd worked for nearly all your life turns out to be not... *all that?*

I was supposed to be preparing a lecture, but my mind was exploring what the fallout would be if, instead of the lecture on nineteenth-century playwrights I was supposed to give, I walked into class and let loose with exactly how I felt about Wellshire

University, academia, students who couldn't give a shit about learning, and all the other symptoms of my terrible case of burnout.

I had no doubt that several students, once they realized their professor had lost his mind, would begin filming me with the phones that were never far from their fingertips. In no time at all, my rant would be viral, shooting through the university hierarchy to the president's office, where a mandate would come down suggesting I look at 'alternatives to Wellshire.'

In other words, *see ya, and don't let the door hit you in the ass on the way out.*

But maybe that was what I wanted.

Going down in flames seemed a heroic exit. Certainly memorable.

But there was the small matter of a mortgage, car payment and various other bills, and the fact that I hadn't published anything in years, that made my university paycheck attractive. Asking if I was ready to give that up was like asking me if I wanted to live on the street.

Or in my car, providing it wasn't repossessed.

But at that moment in time, I had a lovely distraction.

"Nice to meet you, Birdie," I said once she'd introduced herself. "Anything I can help you with?"

Get a grip, asshole.

"I... don't think so, but thank you for asking," she said politely, twirling a stray curl around her finger and looking around the office.

"Are you sure?" I asked warmly. "I'm an English professor, too."

She sighed. "I had hoped to discuss one of my papers with Professor Blake."

I leaned back, elbow on my desk. "I'd be happy to have a look at it if you wanted some constructive criticism. Or maybe an edit?"

She pressed her lips together. I wanted to encourage her further without being a total creep about it. Not sure I was succeeding.

So I just went for it. "May I take a look at your paper, Birdie?"

"I actually already turned it in," she said with a shrug. "So, it's too late for editing or anything like that."

I cleaned my glasses with the corner of my shirt and cocked my head. "If you don't mind my asking, what issue did you want to discuss with Professor Blake, then?"

She paused for a moment. "It was… it was the assignment to write about something that's easy for other people, but not for us. Anyway, after I turned it in and I got to talking with my roommate about it I realized the content was just too personal. I should never have shared that I'm… well, I have an issue that most other students don't."

It was killing me to pretend I didn't know what she was talking about.

"Oh, I've heard about that assignment. Cary—I mean Professor Blake—assigns it every year. Says it really helps students think critically about their place in the world around them. I've read a few papers from his top students. They are very interesting."

"I'll bet they're interesting," she muttered.

"What was that, Birdie?" I asked.

She straightened up in her seat. "I just wish I could withdraw the paper, or whatever you call it, and turn in something else. Even if it meant a grade reduction."

I felt for her. I really did. And I hated that she was embarrassed of her… status.

But I was also puzzled. She was too beautiful to not have a legion of suitors.

And those *lips...*

I shifted in my seat and turned slightly away from her. She didn't need to know the effect she was having on me, which was getting more obvious by the moment.

"Well, Birdie, I can't offer you anything like attorney-client privilege," I laughed, "but I can assure you that anything discussed here won't leave this room. If you want to explore the essay or how Cary might react to it, I'm happy to help."

"Thanks, but I guess it's too late. I just need to put the whole thing behind me."

While the poor girl suffered, my mind wandered over how she would react if I took her face in my hands and kissed her sweet mouth, which I now couldn't tear my gaze from.

Even her crooked teeth were perfect.

Dammit.

"Hey, Birdie, I'm preparing for a lecture at the moment and need to get back to it."

More like, I needed my raging hard-on to subside. Otherwise, I'd be taking myself to the men's room for a quick rub-out.

She jumped to her feet, her little tits quivering the smallest amount. "Oh. Sorry about that. Of course. You have work to do."

"No worries. But hey, would you like to continue this conversation over a cup of coffee sometime?"

Her head twitched the slightest bit, her mouth opening and closing without a word.

I understood. I'd thrown her for a loop.

So I sweetened the deal. Or, tried to. "I can offer you a unique perspective on your future studies with Cary Blake. And the coffee shop I'm thinking of has great scones."

She inched toward the door. "Thank you, but I drink too much coffee as it is," she said, wearing a deer in the headlights look. "And I've taken up too much of your time, I'm sorry."

Well, shit. I should have kept my damn mouth shut.

But just before she let herself out, she dropped a little bomb.

"By the way, Professor Vale, I loved the ending of your book, *Three Seasons in Scarsdale*. It was perfect. Christine deserved so much better than Henrik."

Well, I'd be damned.

Three Seasons was the first novel I'd ever published, and five years later, it still had a small but devoted following. Besides her smile leaving my heart racing, the fact that she'd read my earliest work and could recite the character names from memory, well, I just about proposed marriage.

I waited a couple minutes after she'd left then peeked out the door to make sure she really was gone. With a copy of *Three Seasons* that I'd pulled off my shelf, I held it in front of my raging hard-on and slipped down to the men's room to take care of business.

7

BIRDIE JOHNSON

"Hey, J."

"Hey, B."

Jessa handed two guys their coffees and change, then turned her full attention on me. As the afternoon shift on the campus coffee cart, she had the medicine I needed to make it through the rest of my day and get some studying done before bed. Despite her insistence that school came easily for me, it didn't happen without late nights and my nose buried in books.

"The usual?" she asked in a hopeful tone, already making my favorite coffee drink.

She knew I was pissed. And she knew me well enough to know I was ready to be over it. She hadn't meant to fuck me up. And to be honest, I didn't need help with that, anyway. I was pretty good at it myself.

"I think I could go for some extra pumps of vanilla."

Pretending everything was normal was our way of

making the peace. We didn't outright apologize. We just relied on meaningless banter.

This time it was about the silliness of my coffee preferences.

"Define *some*," she said with a conspiratorial smile.

"Three… or four?" I winced, waiting for her lecture.

Jessa rolled her eyes. "If you want a milkshake, you can get one in the student union." She pointed toward the ice cream shop that, according to its sign, had served Wellshire students for over seventy years.

"I love coffee, but I hate the way it tastes," I complained.

"Okay, well first, that makes no sense. And second, why don't I just fill the cup three quarters of the way with vanilla and add a splash of coffee?" She passed me my drink while shaking her head. I knew my coffee habit killed her, a real java aficionado.

"Even a middle school kid could handle something stronger than this."

"You know, criticizing your customers probably isn't the best way to grow your tips."

But it was worth taking her crap for all the free coffee I got.

"I never criticize customers who actually tip!" she laughed.

She looked over my shoulder. "Oh! Don't look now, but there's a hottie headed our way. He'll probably tip, and definitely get my number if he wants it."

I glanced over my shoulder and about spit out the

first mouthful of obscenely sweet coffee I'd just sucked through my drink stirrer.

Professor Leo Vale was headed straight for us.

"Hello, Birdie. Twice in one day," he called as he spotted me.

Jessa's mouth hung open, and her eyes widened. I played it as cool as I could, but inside I was freaking out a little. *Was he following me? Stalking me? Would I mind if he were?*

"Hi, Professor Vale," I said with a smile. "Serendipity, right?"

"For sure," he said, barely taking his eyes off me.

Jessa cleared her throat, and I snapped back to attention.

"This is Jessa, my roommate," I said.

He waved a hand in the air. "Please, call me Leo," he said, reaching to shake hands with her.

He looked between the two of us. "So you are roommates? Now I see what you mean by getting plenty of coffee."

"What can I get for you Prof… I mean, Leo?" Jessa asked, batting her eyelashes.

Really?

He either didn't notice, or pretended not to. "Just a coffee, Jessa, straight up."

"On the house," she said, handing it to him.

"If you're trying to improve your grade in my class with a bribe, I'm afraid you'll have to sign up for one of my classes first," he joked, stuffing a fiver in her tip jar.

Smart girl.

"Friends and family discount," Jessa explained. "If you're okay with Birdie, you're okay with me."

"Thanks," he said, lifting his cup and turning to leave. But he paused and turned back. "Hey Birdie, have you thought about what you might do about that paper?"

Ugh. The paper.

"Hope for the best?" I shrugged.

"I'm certain Cary will grade it fairly and I doubt he'll be surprised by anything in it. He's been at this teaching thing for a few years."

Wait a minute.

Had he read my paper? Did he know what I was talking about the whole time I was cringing under his gaze? I mean, he shared an office with Professor Blake, and the TA, too. If they talked at all, and I was sure they did, were they having a laugh at my expense?

Fuckers. Now I was getting pissed. Again.

Hours later I met Jessa for dinner at the dining hall.

"Call me *Leo*," she teased in her deepest possible voice after we'd filled our trays with something resembling chicken. "Damn if that man wasn't hot. Hope he comes by my cart again."

"He asked me out for coffee," I casually mentioned.

She dropped her fork, and her jaw followed. "What?"

"Yeah. He suggested we discuss my paper, and strategies for success in Professor Blake's class," I said, although I couldn't help but wonder if it was typical for one professor to offer advice for getting through another professor's course.

Jessa saw through it right away. I was a little slower with these things.

"*Ostensibly* to talk about that stuff," she said. "He can discuss that shit all day long without leaving his office. If he asked you out to coffee, he was *asking you out.*"

"*Me?*"

"Hello? Earth to Birdie. Come in, please," she said, rolling her eyes.

"He *is* handsome. And when I was talking to him in his office there was…an attraction or something. Wait. No. There's no way. He's not interested in me."

"Why not?"

I shrugged. I didn't have an answer.

"How old do you think he is?" she asked.

"Hmmm. I hadn't really thought about it, but I'd guess thirties? Same with Professor Blake. But I think his TA, Kai, is just a couple years older than us."

"He sure is in good shape." Jessa paused, then looked at me with surprise. "Oh my God. Birdie, what if he read your paper? What if he read your paper and he wants to, you know…?"

My thought exactly.

"He wants to be the one. Your first. Which, if I'm

being honest, sounds amazing, since he would actually probably take his time and not be completely awful like my first and every other girl who gave it up on prom night."

I let that soak into my thoughts for a minute while a different part of my body entertained the idea of sleeping with a handsome older man. A strange heat washed over my face and I was feeling very tingly down *there*.

"I never really thought about older men much," I said while mulling over just how big a mistake it might be to hook up with a professor, as if that were even on the table.

Jessa drummed her fingers. "Bullshit. You're telling me your dad never had a buddy who was a little extra-friendly with you? Or one of your friends had a hot dad who made you wonder? Who looked at you a certain way?"

"No. Nope. Absolutely not," I lied as we got up to head back to the dorm.

I couldn't deny that Jessa had hit a nerve. It always seemed wrong somehow, but I absolutely knew what she was talking about. I just didn't realize anybody else had the same sorts of feelings.

On the way into our room, she brought it up again.

"All I know is that Leo Vale can have free coffee at my cart anytime. And if you don't want to, I'll be more than happy to hang out with him."

I was about to tell her he was all hers when our

neighbor, the sex queen started up, and drown me out with sounds that echoed up and down our hallway.

8

PROFESSOR CARY BLAKE

AS I WALKED to class that morning, I recalled how my hopes and expectations had changed the longer I taught college English.

Over time, it became apparent that Wellshire was unlikely to produce any giants of the literary world, so I began to hope for classes filled with interesting students. Even if they weren't supremely talented, they could challenge me with their perspectives. When that didn't happen, I lowered the bar yet again and hoped that each class might contain one, just *one* student I looked forward to seeing each day. It didn't seem like too much to ask.

Birdie Johnson was that one for my ten a.m. Not that I ever heard much from her in class, but her school work was insightful, and more than that, she had a look and an energy about her that was more than alluring. It was downright captivating.

My mind wandered back to watching her walk into

the psychology building, and how even though she showed almost no skin and made no outward attempt to gain my, or anyone else's attention, I couldn't take my eyes off her, even as three of Wellshire's most classic beauties giggled and jiggled and practically offered to blow me right there in front of the entire student body.

Later that night, I found my hand on my hard cock, imagining Birdie's soft curls falling around my face as she rode me, and my quick explosion was beyond anything any of those three plastics could ever have given me.

I'd been mildly intrigued by her, but when she opened up in her essay and really laid bare what she thought were her shortcomings, well I had to say I saw her in a completely new light. She had no idea what she had going for her—brains and beauty were one of the most powerful combinations on earth and she had endless amounts of both.

And not a goddamn thing to be ashamed of. I was going to let her know that, first chance I got.

As I began my lecture, my eyes went right past the bare legs and tight tops of the front row girls, finding their way to Birdie and those lips of hers. The stirring beneath my belt was something I thought I could handle, but the more I glanced at her, the more obvious it became that I needed to take a seat behind the large classroom desk to hide my now-rock-hard cock. I normally liked to walk around during my lectures, making notes on the board and interacting with the students, so sitting down was out of character for me. But if anyone picked up on the change, they didn't show it.

Jesus, I hadn't had hard-ons like this since first meeting my wife.

Ex-wife, that is.

Despite my frequent glances, not once did Birdie meet my gaze. I knew she tended to be on the shy side anyway, but c'mon. At least look my way.

It was a no go.

That said, I hoped what I'd written on her graded essay wouldn't make her crawl under her desk and hide. I considered it part of my job to encourage my students in new directions, past fears and self-imposed limitations. That's what I hoped to do with Birdie.

Okay, maybe it wasn't all quite so noble. I couldn't lie. I wouldn't have minded more, as unlikely as it was for me to get involved with a student.

Write as if you accomplished what you hadn't in this essay. How does it feel? How does it change you?

Those were the words I scrawled in red ink just below the *A+, well done* mark I'd given her.

I was dying for her to reveal more about herself, so I'd tried to give her the forum to do so.

Once my erection was under control, I handed back the graded papers and announced the next assignment. "On each of your papers you'll find a grade and notes, including a follow-up assignment based on what you've written. Some will be different from others, at my discretion, based on what you've written in the first essay."

As I finished, I arrived at Birdie's desk, having put her paper at the bottom of the pile so I could pass hers out last. Her initial smile at seeing her top grade quickly became serious as her cheeks flushed a bright pink.

She glanced up and smiled nervously at me, looked down at the paper again, and smiled more confidently.

Had I just opened Pandora's Box?

After a busy day of classes and office hours, I met Leo at the gym. We had a half marathon coming up, and while I knew I could complete it without a problem, I needed more training time.

We started out in the weight room, arguing about who Wellshire might hire to replace the men's basketball coach, who'd been fired earlier in the week after a third consecutive season of disappointing results. One of the candidates was a former student of mine who just retired from playing pro ball in Europe. It would be cool as hell if he got the job.

As coeds kept popping by to flirt with one or both of us, it started to become clear that the campus rumor mill was going full bore with news of my divorce from Joan. I'd always kept my students at arm's length, especially after I got married. Leo had always been on the same page, well aware of how sticky a situation sleeping with a student could become, but each year they became more brazen, and my change in marital status was like blood in the water.

I looked up at Leo as he spotted me on the bench press. "Hey, did I tell you I met the virgin?" he asked.

Heads turned in our direction, and he was lucky I didn't drop my weight on his foot. Accidentally on purpose.

Teeth gritted, I powered through the last three presses. "Save it for the track, big mouth, I don't want anybody to hear about her," I hissed.

He laughed. "Didn't know she meant that much to you, my friend."

"For fuck's sake, Leo, the last thing we need is somebody to overhear us discussing a student's sex life."

"Or lack thereof," he corrected, the need for discretion having quieted him some.

"Either way," I said, toweling off my face before we headed to the track.

We started with an easy pace, as Leo told me how Birdie had come to the office looking for me and how he'd later bumped into her at the coffee cart.

"I need to patronize the cart. My neighborhood coffee shop never gets my order right," I said, shaking my head.

I told him what I'd written on her essay, hoping to coax more out of her. Obviously, I left out the part about masturbating to the thought of her solving her problem on the end of my dick.

"What is it about her, do you think?" I asked, increasing the pace.

"She's smart," Leo said.

"Lots of smart young women around here," I replied.

"I wasn't finished," Leo answered. "She's, I don't know, *fresh*."

"Because she's a virgin?"

"No, if she'd had a hundred partners, it wouldn't change anything. The way she looks, her flawless skin, those curls..."

"It's her mouth," I commented. "I can't stop staring at it. And thinking about how those lips would feel..."

Now it was Leo's turn to quicken the pace, as my body tried to decide whether it was supposed to send more energy to my legs and lungs or to my stiffening dick.

"You can't have missed her ass," Leo observed.

"That's what's wild," I said. "Half the girls in my classes wear yoga pants and skimpy shorts and do everything they can to accentuate what they've got, but Birdie just shows up like *hey, this is me* and she blows them all out of the water."

"It would be a fucking shame if some drunk frat bro was her first. Some two-pump chump who couldn't find her clit with a map, who just wants to drop his load before he passes out," he said.

I nodded and dug deep to increase my speed. As we

rounded the bend toward the finish line, my sudden burst caught Leo off-guard. I left him ten yards behind me and then walked in circles, hands behind my head.

"Sounds as if you intend to make a move on young Miss Birdie Johnson," Leo said.

A group of three sorority girls jogged past, smiling and waving.

Once they were out of earshot, I answered. "I was just about to say the same about you."

As we walked a cooldown lap, Leo offered his hand to me. I shook it. "Let's wait for her next essay and maybe it'll give us a hint of how to proceed. We need to get a sense of her interest."

"There's just one thing," I said as we headed toward the shower.

"Yeah?"

"Kai is… interested, too."

Leo's eyes grew wide. "Hot damn. Well, I'm not a possessive guy. Let him take his shot."

But not until after I'd had mine.

9

BIRDIE JOHNSON

THE LIBRARY HAD BEEN BORING all afternoon. No noisy sex or even quiet sex, none of the students had the decency to leave any reference materials lying around for me to reshelve, and the computers were all working perfectly. Even though I really counted on the spending money I earned at my part-time job, I was hoping the boss might tell me to clock out early. But with Angelo home with a stomach bug, I figured I'd be stuck there until closing time.

I had just finished the satisfying task of refilling one of the copiers with paper when I noticed Professor Blake come in, scanning the room as if he were looking for someone.

Shit. I did not want to chat with him.

As his head swiveled, I ducked behind the shelves. He took a seat at an empty table, checked his watch, and began scrolling through his phone. Luckily his back was to me, and I was able to sneak over to the information desk to retrieve some books for reshelving.

Moments later, a beautiful woman walked in, tall and elegant with close-cropped hair. There weren't many patrons in the library, but those who were there stared and gawked.

She marched directly to the table where Professor Blake sat, and he rose to greet her with a hug. I watched them talking and laughing from too far away to actually hear them. To my surprise, a heavy stone of sadness settled in my belly.

Strange. I hadn't expected that.

Cary Blake was an accomplished and attractive man, so I should have assumed he'd have a significant other now that he was divorced, but to actually see her up close like this left me… *disappointed.* Not that I could blame him. The woman was a goddess, and the way the guys in the library broke their necks to watch her walk across the room made me confident that they'd all participate in a no-holds-barred death match if the grand prize was a night with her.

Had part of me had fooled myself into thinking there was a chance for little old me, plain Jane Birdie Johnson, with the glamorous Professor Cary Blake? But that wasn't to be. It was just as well anyway.

I watched them for a while, and the way she kept touching his arm and easily laughing just cemented how attached they were. I busied myself with straightening and restocking shelves and did paperwork for a reference book a student had returned with a chunk of twenty-to-thirty pages ripped out of it.

Asshole.

Then I printed out a list of hold requests and got on the elevator to head upstairs. But a hand blocked the closing doors and a man got on.

Professor Cary Blake.

"Hello, Birdie, he said in a surprised voice. "Hadn't realized you were working today."

"Hi, Professor Blake," I stammered. "Yeah, you can usually find me here, whether it's working or studying."

"One of my favorite places on campus," he said.

I pretended to study my holds list, but my mouth would have none of it. "Did your girlfriend leave?" I blurted out.

Jesus, what was wrong with me?

"My what?" Professor Blake asked. "Girlfriend? I don't have a girlfriend."

"Sorry, that woman you were with downstairs," I said as we exited the elevator together. "Your girl-friend? Or wife?"

He looked at me with confusion then laughed, a bit too loud for the library. I raised a finger to my lips to remind him where we were.

"Sorry," he said with a chuckle. "You must mean Ivonna. She's my trainer. I'm running a half marathon later this month, and she's coaching me. She ran track here years ago and was a student of mine. She almost made the Olympic team. She's fantastic."

Oh. Well. And now I was a nosy stalker.

"She's very… impressive," I agreed. "Everybody stopped what they were doing when she walked in."

"Ivonna is quite beautiful," he said, "But we're not an item. I'm not at all her type."

I could see her with a movie star or an NBA player, but I found it hard to imagine any woman flatly turning down Cary Blake as 'not their type.'

He evidently read the confusion on my face. "If you're single, you should ask her out," he suggested with a laugh. "You'd have a much better shot than I would."

If I'm single? I just poured my heart out over fourteen hundred words about how single I am.

"Ivonna is a lesbian," he clarified.

"Ohhhh," I said, hitting my forehead with the heel of my hand. "Duh."

"Professor Blake, I can't have you monopolizing my employees," came the shrill voice of my boss.

Leave it to that woman to cock-block me.

"I need Miss Johnson to pull those holds for me, Professor. Is there something I can help you with?"

"Not at all. Birdie is one of my students, and we were just discussing an assignment. I'm looking for the new poetry collection if it's in."

"First floor," she said with fake exasperation. "Now shoo!"

Professor Blake headed back to the elevator. "See you in class, Birdie."

I waved and scurried off to retrieve the holds,

relieved that we hadn't ventured into the territory of the assignment he'd suggested I write next. I had no idea how to tackle it. And I knew I didn't want to talk about it. At least not with him.

Back in the dorm, I collapsed on my bed, hopeful that Jessa had remembered her promise to bring me a to-go bag from the dining hall, since I'd worked past closing time.

Shortly after, Jessa and Roxy, joined at the hip like always, popped into the room with a big salad exactly how I liked it.

"You guys are goddesses. Thank you so much," I said, ready to inhale my food.

We talked about a guy Roxy had been seeing casually in between her shifts as a maid at a local hotel, a band Jessa wanted to follow to festivals over the summer, and what a creep Professor Hartsell in the history department was.

I had just finished my salad when Roxy cautiously asked about my 'virgin paper.'

But she needn't worry. I didn't blame her or Jessa for their... suggestion that I write it.

"I got an A+, so that's cool, but now we have a new assignment, that's sort of a sequel to the first."

"How so?" Jessa asked.

I fished the paper out of my backpack and read the new assignment aloud—*Write as if you accomplished what you hadn't in this essay. How does it feel? How does it change you?*

I tossed the paper onto my desk. "How the hell am I supposed to write that? If I've never had sex, how would I know?"

"Get sex goddess next door to write it for you," Jessa said.

That again. No way would I ever risk my scholarship and college career by doing something like that.

She continued. "Nobody has more sex than she does. On the other hand, she probably doesn't remember what it was like to be a virgin, so it probably won't get you another A+."

So. Funny.

"No, I'll write… something. I just don't know what."

"That's such a weird assignment. Applied to anybody's essay it would be weird, but especially to yours. I had that class last semester, and I don't recall having a follow-up like that."

Roxy jumped to her feet with a professorial finger in the air. "How does it feel? Major disappointment. And how does it change you? You wonder why everybody makes such a big deal about something that's quick, painful, and awful."

Jessa laughed and nodded her head.

"Sex is awful?" I asked.

"The first time," Jessa said, "for me and for Roxy, like a lot of girls, was in high school. We had very similar experiences. Guys who had no idea what they were doing, who could hardly get it in before they finished, and who did absolutely nothing to help us get any enjoyment out of it aside from biting our necks. Awful. But no, generally speaking, sex is not awful."

Roxy jumped in. "The problem is that most guys, high school and college guys at least, look at sex as a spring to see how fast they can have an orgasm. And then they're done. Whether that means rolling over and going to sleep or up and leaving. So yeah, it can be good while it lasts, but it's like give an average guy ten blowjobs and he'll return the favor by going down on you for thirty seconds. Whoop-de-damn-doo."

Jesus. I didn't get what all the fuss was about.

"That's a good way of looking at it," Jessa said. "For guys sex is a sprint, for us it's a marathon, so it can be hard to find that middle ground where everybody's happy. Unless you're considering an older, more experienced man," she taunted.

I pretended I had no idea what she was talking about. "I could probably BS my way through an essay, but I wish it could be more than that. How am I supposed to write a realistic essay about the aftermath of losing my V card without... losing my V card?"

KAI FLEMINSTER

"Just a minute."

I shoved the bag of chips I'd been eating into a drawer, stood up, and wiped my shirt free of crumbs.

I'd been trying to kill two of the most boring hours of my life, sitting in for Professor Blake's weekly office hours while he and Professor Kale were out glad-handing it with some big university donors. And while I dragged my ass through the impossible *Ulysses*, required reading by my PhD advisor, the only thing that could possibly make the afternoon worse was an actual student coming by to talk.

Which was the whole reason I was there. But it didn't mean I was excited to have company.

When the knock on the door came, I groaned, only cutting myself off when I realized my protest could probably be heard in the hallway. I thought for a moment about pretending not to be in, but because I'd been such a noisy idiot, and because it would also piss

Blake off royally, I sucked it up and walked to the door where I expected a clueless undergrad begging for a better grade with no plan to actually do the work required.

I shouldn't talk though. I'd been a bit of a punk in my undergrad days, myself. I mean, what college student wanted to do a bit more work than he or she absolutely had to? The whole experience was so much more than books and grades.

It was a miracle I'd been accepted into grad school, family connections notwithstanding.

So I pulled open the door, bravely ready to face a mirror image of what I'd been only a few years earlier when drinking beer and getting laid were my top priorities in life.

But no.

Who stood there but the lovely Birdie Johnson. College virgin. And to be honest, object of my nightly dreams ever since I'd read her A+ essay.

I cleared my throat and ran my fingers over my beard, hoping to remove any errant Dorito crumbs, and stepped aside to let her enter.

My day was looking up. I glanced over at the blasted *Ulysses* to mock its ability to cause misery.

Not today, bitch.

"Birdie. Nice to see you," I gushed, brushing against a pile of papers that went flying to the floor.

Jesus. Control yourself, asshole.

"Hi, Kai. I was just looking for Professor Blake.

Guess I missed him?" she asked, bending to help me pick things up.

She handed me her stack of papers, but not before stealing a quick glance at them. "Seems like I'm always helping you pick things up, doesn't it?"

She smiled at me. And goddamn if she wasn't cute.

"It does seem like that, doesn't it?"

She pointed at the stack, which I'd returned to the corner of Blake's desk. Face down.

But it was too late.

"Hey, Kai, are those papers from one of Professor Blake's classes?" she asked.

"Yeah. I think from his eight a.m."

She pressed her lips together and a small worry line creased her forehead. "Um, well, do you read those papers? Or does the professor?"

Oh shit. I knew exactly what she was going after.

Might as well come clean.

I stuffed my hands deep in my pockets and rocked on my feet to play it cool. "Well, the way we work is I do the first pass on the papers and make notes. Then he does the second pass and we discuss them together. Well, we discuss most of them. Some are so bad there's nothing to talk about."

Damn. Had I really just said that?

So I doubled over at the waist and burst out laughing, trying to fake a joke.

But I don't think I fooled her.

Her face paled. "Oh. Well. Does... does anybody else

read our papers?" she asked, her voice ending in a squeak.

I hated that she was struggling with this whole thing. Thinking back to the quiet desperation of her essay and how she felt surrounded by so much sex—and how I'd read between the lines and guessed how badly she needed some of her own—I wanted to soothe her in the best way I knew how.

But that wouldn't be cool.

Right?

My cock seemed to feel differently however, and I plopped down at my desk to hide my growing erection.

"Well, Birdie, sometimes Professor Vale reads the papers, too. Just the really good ones, though."

Oh fuck. I did it again.

And now she knew. The three of us clowns, probably the last people on earth she wanted to know her personal business, were now acquainted with her deepest, darkest secret.

I thought I might change the subject.

"So, Birdie, what can I do for you today? Blake and Vale are out with the university president, probably drinking good champagne and eating caviar."

While I suffered in their cramped, dusty office with *Ulysses*.

But hey, I had Birdie.

"Oh. Right," she said, remembering the initial purpose of her visit. "It's this latest assignment I got from Professor Blake. Now I have to write as if I'd accomplished the one thing I couldn't, and expand on how it felt and how it changed me."

I nodded, not letting on I already knew about Birdie's 'special' assignment. No, I kept that to myself as well as the fact that it was the first time Blake had ever even assigned a follow up like that.

She didn't need to know that bit.

So I crossed my arms, nodding as professorially as I could. "Yeah. That's tough, Birdie. I can see how that could be tricky, writing about what you feel is your biggest challenge suddenly getting reversed. I mean, how the hell is that supposed to work?" I asked, shaking my head to let her know I was on her side.

She nodded hopefully. "See what I mean?"

Fuck me. Her eyes were wide with fear. Fear that she couldn't complete an assignment, which was about the worst thing in the world for a straight-A student.

Not that I knew firsthand. But I had a smart roommate sophomore year. The agony that guy went through over his grades had been hard to watch.

"I might be able to help. Refresh my memory, what was your first essay about?"

I knew full well what it was about. And she knew I knew what it was about. What she didn't know was that I'd read it half a dozen times. Nor did she know I'd jerked off to thoughts of her pretty face at least twice that much.

She sighed, and I waited for her to call me out. But, there was the slightest little twinkle in her eye.

It was hot as fuck.

She looked at me. Hard. And she twisted one of the curls hanging down in front of her shoulder.

"Um… okay. I wrote about…"

I bit the inside of my cheek to maintain my poker face.

"I wrote about how everybody at Wellshire University is having sex," she blurted out, just like we both knew she would. And she didn't stop there. "Like, all the time and everywhere. In the dorms. In the library. In their cars. Everybody. All the time. Except me and that's not going to change anytime soon. So how am I supposed to write about what it's like to have had sex when I've only even kissed a couple guys?"

I was speechless. Fucking speechless.

Which I think made her feel even worse. The rims of her eyes got red and sparkly with tears.

So I acted like nothing was out of place.

"Oh yeah, I remember your essay now," I said with a casual wave of my hand.

Jesus. I hadn't been able to forget it.

"You did a great job, Birdie. It was very well-written. Very brave."

She exhaled and smiled half-heartedly.

"If you don't mind me asking, did you grow up super religious or something?" I asked.

"No, why?"

"It's just that… you're so beautiful. You could have any guy you wanted on this or any other campus. It makes the whole thing hard to figure. I believe you, your paper was completely authentic, but it's like somebody who works in a candy factory saying they've never tasted chocolate."

There. I'd said it. While I had no doubt her paper had been honest, when it came down to it, it was still hard to believe.

She shifted in her seat, avoiding my gaze. "Thanks for the compliment. You're very kind. But seriously. Kai, there's nothing special about me."

"That's where you're wrong," I said matter-of-factly.

If we were already crossing the line, I might as well go all the way, I figured.

"This might sound strange, Birdie, but what about watching porn?"

I didn't know if she was going to slap me across the face or ask for the best porn website for free content.

So I kept talking. "You know, for research purposes. There are tons of free porn sites on the internet. YouPorn, PornHub, etcetera. Maybe they can give you some ideas of, you know, what to write about? Get those creative juices flowing?"

Or get something flowing. Jesus, my dick was hard as a rock.

She pressed her lips together again and nodded slowly. "That's... just crazy enough to be a good idea."

Yes.

Before I opened my big mouth and offered to watch porn with her, the office phone, one of the only land lines I'd used in years, rang. A small press publisher wanted to know if Professor Blake would be interested in curating a collection of short stories by local authors. I held up a hand to keep Birdie in the room while I made a note for Blake.

She got to her feet and slung her backpack over her shoulder when I hung up. "Thanks for your help. And for the compliment. I'm not… used to them."

I walked around the desk to meet her by the door.

"You deserve to hear them all the time," I said, looking down into her eyes. There was a tension as we stood so close, my hand on the doorknob, the turn of which would end whatever was happening between us.

Without thinking about it, because if I *did* think about it, I never would have acted, I released the doorknob and wove my fingers through her wild hair. "It's criminal that lips like yours aren't being kissed constantly."

I leaned down to kiss her, and after hesitating only for a moment, she leaned into me, her backpack crashing to the floor.

I cradled her face as we kissed, her lips softer and sweeter than I'd even imagined.

I pulled back, licking my lips for any remaining taste of her. ""Will that help with your essay?" I asked.

"I… think it will, yes," she said, slipping out the door with a smile.

And she was gone.

She left me throbbing, searching the room for any hint of her scent.

I sat for a while, thinking about her and where our kiss might lead, but at the same time recalling the many warnings my father and grandfather gave me about a teacher/student relationship.

Office hours over, I was packing up my things when Blake returned and found me deep in thought.

"I got a question for you, Cary. How do you handle pretty students?" I asked. "Being attracted to them, and all?"

He stopped what he was doing and turned to face me with a look of surprise. I didn't care if he knew. I wanted him to.

"First off, it's a college campus. Unless you're blind or asexual, you're eventually going to wind up attracted to someone. These students are people in the prime of their lives. They're young, beautiful, and exciting. It's inevitable. And second, are you speaking of anyone in particular? Or just generally?"

I ignored his question for a moment. "What about acting on it? How do you... resist? What if you... can't?"

"What's on your mind, Kai?" he asked, hands on hips.

I took a deep breath, hoping he wouldn't fire my ass for being proactive. "Birdie. Birdie Johnson. The virgin. She came by looking for you, to talk about the follow-up assignment. And we may have... well, we kissed. And I don't think I regret it."

He stared at me before he spoke. "She might just be trouble for all of us. She's... well, fucking irresistible. I thought about kissing her in the elevator at the library the other day."

Knowing I was not the only one was strangely comforting.

I wasn't alone.

"What about Leo?" I asked.

What the hell. Let's lay it all out.

Blake nodded. "Yup. Him too."

Holy fuck.

All three of us had the hots for the pretty virgin. The pretty, smart, modest, interesting virgin.

I sank back into my chair, shocked but not shocked.

Why shouldn't the three of us be attracted to Birdie? We had a lot in common, and that evidently extended to what we valued in women.

But what did it mean?

"Kai, you should ask her out. I intend to. I can't stop thinking about her."

"Seriously?" I had a feeling he'd say something like that, but when the words were spoken out loud, it sounded more outlandish than it had in my thoughts.

"Leo plans to ask her out, as well. Look, what you do is up to you, but I'm not discouraging you. I have a feeling about that girl, and she may be too much for any of the three of us."

Maybe so. But I sure planned to find out.

11

BIRDIE JOHNSON

WHAT THE HELL had just happened?

I'd kissed a TA. In my professor's office. A guy I barely knew.

He was just a TA, it was true, but TAs were essentially professors-in-training.

So. Not. Cool.

And... I'd liked it. Yes, I'd liked it. A lot. And I was prepared to do more before I forced myself to get the hell out of there, run down the hall like an idiot, and hightail it back to my dorm like a freaking little kid running home to mommy.

Or, like a scared virgin.

Either way.

My body was totally into the kiss, as surprising and completely out-of-nowhere as it was, and I craved more. More kissing and more... *stuff*. My mind, on the other hand, was screaming the entire time to get out of there fast, and to preserve the academic record I'd worked so hard to compile, the reputation I'd so carefully cultivated…

Wait a minute.

Wasn't my *reputation*, my entire persona, Birdie Johnson, virgin brainiac, the entire problem in the first place?

And now, rather than being the super-studious, eternally single Birdie Johnson, here I was kissing a guy and having a massive crush on two others, who just all happened to be academics, sharing an office, in the English department, where I had my major. Where I also had a partial scholarship, which had been a huge relief to my parents.

Shoot me now.

None of the thousands of guys my age, on campus or otherwise, showed me any romantic or sexual interest, and I reciprocated the feeling, aggressively. They seemed so juvenile. It was all frat parties and beer pong and football and 'Megan Thee Stallion is so hot!' and Xbox and… *yuck.*

But Professors Blake and Vale, and the TA Kai, were so different. Mature, quietly confident, gorgeous, smart, accomplished, and sexy as hell.

I had to stop thinking about them, though. Just because Kai had kissed me didn't mean a damn thing, no matter how much I'd liked it. The bottom line was that none of them would get involved with me because one, they just wouldn't be interested in someone like me, and two, because I was a freaking student. Duh.

Even though they knew I was the only virgin for miles. Which probably was an exaggeration, but still.

I entered my room to find Jessa dancing with her earbuds in, and I laughed through her embarrassment while she caught her breath.

"What's up with you, you're acting weird," she said when she'd chugged a bottle of water.

"I'm weird? You're the one dancing like you have ants in your pants."

"It's the new Dua Lipa song. I just love it. And anyway, dancing saves me a trip to the gym. But yeah, you have a secret. I can tell," she said, shaking a finger in my face.

Damn her, she knew me too well.

In spite of that, I considered denying it. But I decided to come clean. Jessa had met Leo and knew all about Blake and Kai and my paper, and even though she was not really at fault for my getting into the predicament I was in, she might be able to help me find a way out.

"Are you sure you want to hear this? I mean, I've stumbled into a mess," I said.

Her eyes widened. I knew I'd get her with that.

She sat down on the edge of her bed, leaning toward me, her mouth hanging open in expectation, like a baby bird hoping to be fed.

"Well, Jessa, I have a… problem on my hands. The word *crush* seems so juvenile, but I can't think of another that fits the situation better."

She gasped. "You have a crush on someone. Oh my

god. Who? Is it that guy who works in the library with you? Angelo?"

I rolled my eyes. "He's gay, Jessa. I've told you that."

She slapped her leg. "Right, right. Okay, keep going."

It was telling that she couldn't name another guy I might have a crush on.

Suddenly, she waved her hands like she'd lost her mind. "Oh my god, Birdie. I knew it. I just knew it. You're a *lesbian*."

"No, that's not it either—"

But she cut me off. "No, no, no, do not be ashamed. You know I'll love and respect you, regardless. I just wish I'd figured it out sooner. No wonder you always stared at the sex queen—"

"Jessa, stop! I am not a lesbian, and if I do stare at the sex queen, it's only because I'm fascinated by her. What I'm trying to tell you is…"

Her face fell. I guess she really wanted me to be a lesbian. Her younger sister was one, and I'd bet a hundred dollars she'd already fixed us up together in her mind.

I mean, I *could* consider a walk on the 'wild side.' But first things first.

"Jessa. Listen. Just listen. For a moment."

She ran her fingers across her lips in the old 'zipping it up' motion. I wasn't convinced that was going to keep her quiet, so I spoke fast.

The words flew out of my mouth. "Jessa, I have a thing for two professors. Blake and Vale. Oh, and I kissed their TA, Kai. Well, he kissed *me*. Okay, *we* kissed."

It took her a moment to respond. "Holy shit, B," she said slowly, staring at me like I had two heads. "The guy with the red hair? Who looks like a cuter version of Prince Harry? Who wears flip flops all year long?"

I nodded. "Yeah. That's him. But it was just a, you know, kiss."

A smile crept over her face. "You could totally hop on his dick. Lose that freaking V-card."

If only it were that easy.

Although, maybe it was.

"Jessa!" I said, feigning shock.

"What? You want to lose it, right? There you go. Perfect opportunity. He's good-looking and smart. What more do you need?"

Oh god.

"I guess it's not like I need more… but maybe I want more. You yourself, and Roxy said you gave it away too freely the first time. Maybe that's not how I want it to be?"

She rolled her eyes. "Oh, c'mon, Birdie, it's not like you're the freaking Virgin Mary. You're not carrying the baby Jesus. Just get it the hell over with and stop tormenting yourself. It's like someone is offering you a lovely filet mignon, and you're stalling, asking if it's organic."

"What? You are so full of shit. I mean, I've never been more ready. These past few days since I wrote that paper have been driving me insane. But all of a sudden, I'm like… I don't know. I can't stop thinking about any of the three of them. I don't know what to do. And don't use a stupid analogy on me like that again," I warned.

But I also laughed.

"Birdie, practically every girl on this and every other campus fantasizes about hooking up with a professor. Older dudes in general, but a professor? It's dirty, taboo, and freaking hot! An authority figure, who has some power over you, being taken down by the vagina. What better fantasy is there? It's like saying 'you can give me a grade, but I can give you a blowjob.' It kind of makes you even, don't you think?"

I wasn't so sure about that…

I put my head in my hands. "I don't know. I always heard the professor/student relationship was kind of predatory. Like the prof was in the driver seat and the student had no say about anything."

Jessa jumped to her feet so fast she scared me. "THAT'S WHAT I'M TALKING ABOUT. Some girls give away their power, sure. But the smart ones don't. In fact, we've got the power. We're the ones who bring them to their knees. Topple governments. Cause feast and famine—"

"Okay, I think you can take it easy now. The hyperbole is getting old," I said.

But she had a point. Problem was, how would I choose? That is, if I were given the option?

She waved a finger in my face. "I've got an idea. Rather than trying to decide among the three, go to the office when they're all there. See what happens. Follow your instinct."

She stood and started doing a sexy hip-chucking walk around the room. "Boom chicka bow wow! No longer Birdie Johnson, virgin. I can see it now," she sang. "Birdie Johnson, sex goddess of Wellshire University, with two professors—wait, two *hot* professors—and a ruggedly handsome TA falling at her feet. You'd be the envy of every girl who ever batted her eyelashes at a professor."

"You have officially lost your mind." I took a seat at my desk to get cracking on my next essay. The impossible one. That I had no idea how to write.

In seconds it became apparent it would be impossible to get any work done with Jessa going on and on about impossible sexual scenarios. So, I excused myself and headed for the library.

I waved to my boss on the way past the library information desk and hustled for the stairs before she had the chance to ask if I could take on any extra shifts. I needed a quiet corner, not only because I was never able to get any work done in the distracting open areas of the library, but also because I wanted a spot where I could do my, um… research.

I walked past the first row of private study rooms,

which were basically not much more than glass-walled telephone booths, finally arriving at an empty one. Because I knew about the shit that went down in the library, I spread a tissue over the chair before I sat and wiped the desk with hand sanitizer.

Obsessive, much?

Taking a deep breath, I opened my laptop. For several minutes, I stared at the blank page and blinking icon, with no idea where to begin.

Nudging my computer aside, I pulled out my phone and pointed my browser to YouPorn, as Kai had suggested. Earbuds in place, I searched 'older man, younger girl' and scrolled through a few selections, pausing to watch a few minutes here and there. Damn.

This shit was no joke.

But it wasn't quite right. Too *wham, bam, thank you ma'am*. Little was sexy or sensual about it. More of an anatomy class than anything.

I went back to the search bar and entered 'older man, younger girl' and even added 'curly hair' for good measure.

Jackpot.

A girl who looked very much like me, around my age with curly dark hair, was naked between two men who had their hands all over her, taking turns kissing her. The guys were in their thirties or forties, with a little graying hair at the temples, the other with salt and pepper scruff on his face.

They were *hot*.

God bless the porn interweb search engines. Why

hadn't I thought to visit here sooner? I'd essentially found myself *and* two of the profs I was thirsting for.

The woman dropped to her knees in front of the two long, thick cocks dueling for her mouth. She sucked them hungrily and before long was riding one while the other used her mouth.

My face burned hot, my thighs pressing tightly together as I watched. I squirmed in my chair, aware that anyone walking by could see me right through the room's glass walls. On the video, the woman's whimpers and moans grew in volume and urgency.

Just like my need.

I considered pursuing my orgasm right then and there, but the smallest sliver of rational thought reigned inside my overheated brain. It wasn't worth the risk, not in a glass-walled room in a library where I freaking worked.

The man who was fucking the girl's face started to come, followed by the one she was riding, and then her own climax hit. My lust boiled over. I slammed my laptop shut and shoved it into my backpack, making a beeline for what I hoped would be the vacant handicapped bathroom in a far corner of the library. Even though my phone was in my pocket, porn noises continued to filter into my brain via my earbuds. I hadn't turned the stupid video off. When it ended, a new one almost immediately started.

Jesus. Is that how this shit worked?

Racewalking across the sprawling library, hoping I wasn't attracting attention, I pushed through the door, locked it behind me, and dropped my pack to the floor. I slumped against the far wall, both hands down the front of my pants, and rubbed frantically. My orgasm arrived with visions of Professor Vale and Professor Blake doing to me what was done to the girl in the video, with Kai thrusting in and out of my one free hand.

It was all I could do to not shriek when my orgasm hit.

Apparently not completely satisfied, I propped my phone on the sink and watched the new video, stroking myself leisurely this time, thinking about the fact that anyone could be right outside the door. They may have seen or heard me, or even be able to *smell* my arousal. I came again, this time watching a 'college basketball player' and a couple of his friends pound a woman in a cheerleader outfit.

I wasn't exactly sure how any of this would help me write my essay, but I felt damn *amazing,* and after composing myself as best I could, I left the restroom.

With the edge taken off, I returned to my glass-walled study room, opened my computer, and got to work.

12

PROFESSOR LEO VALE

SOMETHING ABOUT BIRDIE JOHNSON had taken hold inside me, like an earworm—one of those blasted songs you couldn't get out of your head. I decided I needed to embrace it, since running away wasn't helping. The thoughts were following at least as fast as I was trying to dodge them.

I had sufficient connections around campus to find out which dorm she lived in, but dropping by a student's room, especially that of a *female* student, would likely bring unwanted attention, and therefore trouble.

Scratch that.

The library seemed my best bet if I intended to 'accidentally' bump into her, so I took a stroll in that direction, also on the lookout for the coffee cart where her roommate worked. Double my chances of finding her, I hoped.

But from a distance I could see that the cart was

staffed by a tall skinny guy, so I pressed on for the library.

My legs protested the quick walk, sore as they were from the marathon training I'd been doing with Cary and Kai. Was I getting too old to keep up? Cary was actually two years older than me, although he often called me 'old man' in deference to my longer tenure at Wellshire.

But that was a bunch of crap. A man in his late thirties like me was still near the peak of his lifetime fitness. I was being a pussy.

I paused at a bench and put a leg up on the end of it, bending down to stretch my hamstrings and stay ahead of the stiffness.

"Hi, Professor Vale," came a voice from behind me, dragging out the 'a' sound in my name.

I turned to see two female students walking toward me. They wore tight workout pants that were more stripper garb than anything, swinging their hips from side to side as they passed. I sent them a disinterested wave and a mumble to discourage any conversation or visiting time. I was on a mission.

As I thought about the disinterested undergrads like these women whom I spent my days trying to teach, my thoughts wandered back to whether I might abandon teaching altogether, relocate to a cabin in the woods somewhere, and live a quiet, solitary life.

But the truth was, I wasn't suited for that either, as romantic and hipster as it sounded. I'd do no better in the middle of nowhere and would probably be a thousand times more miserable than I already was, standing in front of a class of students every day who couldn't bother to pay attention to a word I was saying.

But I knew of one way to brighten my day, and I was going to do something about it.

I entered the library and took a look around. No Birdie, but the place was massive, and she could be anywhere. I walked over to the information desk and inquired as to whether anyone had seen her.

A polite woman answered me. "She's off work today, but I saw her just a bit ago, probably here to study. Try the second floor. She usually goes there."

I grabbed the elevator in the interest of preserving my legs and wound around the periphery of the floor, hoping I'd bump into her.

"Professor Vale, Professor Vale," came the same voice from earlier. I turned to find the girls from outside waving me over to their table.

I sighed before approaching them.

"Come sit with us, Professor Vale," the taller one pleaded. She'd removed the hoodie she'd been wearing and was now displaying a pile of cleavage to go with her painted-on pants.

Another time I might have appreciated these young women's assets. Today I could not have been less interested. But that was fine. There'd be plenty other guys who'd fall over themselves to have a five-minute conversation with them.

"What can I do for you ladies?" I asked. They were in one of my classes, but I was hard-pressed to recall either of their names. Or whether they'd ever turned in any of their work on time.

"Oh Professor, we need some *special* tutoring," the shorter one offered. "Like, one on one. Or two on one. We're both struggling with your class. Can you help?" she pouted.

"Maybe if you did the assigned reading," I said under my breath.

"Wish I could," I told them, looking around and spotting Birdie through the glass door of one of the study rooms. "I have a previous engagement."

They'd seen me spot Birdie, and made faces as if they'd just smelled something awful.

"Like *she* needs help," the short one said.

"Oh, she definitely needs help," the taller girl responded. "*Such* a weirdo."

They laughed and high-fived each other across the table.

Fuck them.

I turned away and strode toward Birdie, stopping short as I noticed she was intently watching something on her phone, which was resting on top of her unopened backpack.

Grabbing a book from the nearest shelf, I sat down and pretended to read. The pair of queen bees I'd left in my wake glared at me for leaving for someone they considered below them in the social pecking order.

As I watched Birdie over the top of my book, I noticed she was blushing deeply and squirming in her chair. She licked her lips and then her mouth hung slightly open, all the while her eyes were riveted to the screen.

At one point, her hand even dipped between her legs and remained there for several seconds before she brought it up and ran it through her hair.

Was she watching what I thought she was? In the library?

No freaking way.

But I spied on her for a few moments more before setting my book down and walking over to her.

"Birdie?" I said, opening the door.

But with earbuds in, she didn't hear me.

I cleared my throat and reached to get into her line of sight, waving my hand.

That caught her attention. She half-jumped, half-fell out of her chair, knocking it over as she stumbled away from the table. Her phone when flying, hitting the carpeted floor, followed by her earbuds, which disappeared under the table.

Our eyes met as a new sound filled the room.

"Oh! Oh! Yes! Give me that big cock, Daddy!" a female voice screamed.

We broke eye contact, turning to her phone screen, which displayed a girthy male appendage impaling a wisp of a girl, while another man stood nearby stroking his giant dick.

Holy fucking shit.

I'd caught her red-handed, watching porn.

All color drained from her face, and she snatched up her phone and backpack, bolting from the room, the video continuing to play. Loudly.

"Fuck me! Fuck me! Never stop fucking meeee..." echoed through the library, leaving a trail of laughter behind her as she ran.

I bent down and scooped up her discarded earbuds before breaking into my own run.

13

BIRDIE JOHNSON

AFTER I'D FINISHED myself off in the library handicapped bathroom and returned to my study room, I realized I wasn't *completely* finished. The same itch that had sent me to the bathroom to begin with returned in minutes.

As a YouPorn novice, I had no idea there were so many options, and with every video I watched there were dozens more suggested. The possibilities were infinite.

This could get dangerous. Damn Kai for suggesting it.

So instead of diving in and tackling the paper hanging over my head like a black cloud, I worked my way through a few more scenarios, oblivious to the library around me.

First, there were two guys on one girl.

Then, two girls on one guy.

Oral. Anal. Gay. Straight. The variety was staggering. I was mesmerized.

Just as I was needing to return to the bathroom for another round with myself, a waving hand and smiling face came into my field of vision.

Professor Leo Vale? What the fuck?

I ejected backwards out and over my chair, my phone flying in one direction and my ear buds going in another, all thanks to my shock. Time stopped, and as my fight or flight response kicked in, *flight* had the final word.

As if my fumbling weren't bad enough, before I could even think, a sound filled the small room that clarified I was doing something I should not have been as the earbuds disconnected and the video blared over the phone speaker.

Leo's eyes widened and confusion crossed his face until he realized the sound was coming from my phone. Where a porn video was loudly playing.

I grabbed all my things and tore through the library like a maniac until I was outside.

That's where I realized I'd never shut the app down. My phone had screamed porn the entire time I'd sprinted through the library.

I staggered in the direction of my dorm, jabbing the screen hard enough to crack the glass as I got the hell off YouPorn.

Of course, the one day I desperately needed one, I wasn't wearing a hoodie, which would have helped hide my face from the rest of the world.

And then there was Leo, whom I most certainly could never face again.

"Birdie? Birdie Johnson? Birdie!"

Shit.

There he stood, the gorgeous professor who'd interrupted my porn reverie, his breath slightly accelerated from running after me.

Why was he running after me anyway? Wasn't it obvious from my graceful exit that I was not up for socializing?

"You left these," he said, placing my earbuds in the palm of my hand.

"Oh. Thank you.

I wedged them into a side pocket of my backpack, hands shaking as my adrenaline crashed. Then, the tears started to fall. I bawled where I stood, my shoulders heaving as everything that had just happened became real.

Leo approached and put an arm around my shoulders. "Birdie, come over here. Sit down with me."

"I have found," he began after we'd sat on a bench for a moment, "that most of the time, the things we are embarrassed about, the things we think other people are thinking about every time they see us, are actually quickly forgotten by everyone else."

I sniffled, and he pulled me closer.

"We all have our own lives happening, our own stresses, and while each of us can recite a litany of humiliations we've personally suffered, we'd have much greater difficulty naming even a handful of times we've experienced someone else suffer a similar moment."

Easy for him to say.

Despite myself, I slumped against him. He was so warm and protective, and smelled so freaking great that I couldn't help myself. It was as if I'd been carrying a great weight, and was now being given permission to offload some, if not all of it.

Not that I needed his permission. I just needed reminding.

After a while, I straightened up and swiveled on the bench to face him.

I suspected he was aware of my 'tell all' essay, but I figured I'd start at the beginning, anyway.

"I wrote an essay for Professor Blake's class, which you might be aware of," I said. "It was about something that comes easy for most people, but not for me. The issue is that I'm a virgin. Everybody on campus is hooking up, and I'm this weird nerdy girl nobody wants."

He sighed. "That is such bullshit. You're one of the most beautiful girls here at Wellshire. You just don't know it yet. There's not a man on campus who wouldn't be fortunate to trade places with me right now, where I have my arm around you and your undivided attention for a few minutes."

"Thank you," I managed to say.

"And, I gotta tell you… I read your essay. It was really good."

I knew it.

"Beyond being well-written," he continued, "I found your honesty refreshing. You should feel no shame. For the paper or for being a virgin. There's nothing wrong with it. You're saving yourself, intentionally or not, for one lucky man."

Or *men*. But I kept that to myself.

"Thanks. You're very kind. And as you probably figured, that's how I ended up watching porn. My next assignment is to figure out what it would be like to… um, well, address my little issue. I thought a video or two would give me something to write about."

"And did it?" he asked.

"I'm not sure yet."

How could I tell him that the only way I could really write my next essay was if I actually, you know, lost my V-card. No porn video, while educational for sure, would take the place of such an experience.

But I didn't want him to think I was propositioning him. So I kept my mouth shut.

And it was a good thing I did, because in the next moment, his lips met mine.

He brushed my mouth at first, then pulled back to look at me, his hands weaving through my hair. He kissed the side of my neck, and I sighed, turning my lips back toward his. I wasn't done. Not by a long shot.

And he clearly picked up on that, because he pressed his lips to mine harder this time, so hard it almost hurt. But I wanted it to hurt. I wanted to feel him and taste him. And I did.

My room was mercifully empty, and I was able to knock out my essay in an hour.

On my way to class the next day, I passed Kai. "Birdie. Good morning," he said.

"Morning to you."

"How's everything? Essay coming together?

"I'm on my way to turn it in now, actually," I said. "I think it turned out pretty well. Thank you for your help. And for suggesting YouPorn. I considered adding a footnote detailing your 'contribution,' but I didn't."

I laughed as I watched Kai's eyebrows arch and his pupils dilate. He started to speak but then stopped.

I patted him on the arm. "Kidding. Gotta run. Don't want to be late. You know how Professor Blake can be such a hard... ass," I said with a grin, leaving him standing there, speechless.

14

PROFESSOR CARY BLAKE

I WATCHED Birdie walk into my class, carrying herself with new confidence. With her head high and her gaze straight ahead, I wondered if maybe the change had been brought about by the loss of her virginity.

I hoped not.

I likewise hoped she wasn't on her way to transforming into one of the bitchy alpha girls who filled the front row with their designer everything, overdone makeup, and my-shit-doesn't-stink attitudes.

Part of what made Birdie so appealing, aside from her unique, natural beauty, was her authentic *cool*, the fact that she didn't need to impress anyone with a label, a sorority affiliation, a boyfriend on the football team, or by pointing out anyone else's perceived flaws. With Birdie, her modesty, brains, and looks were all it took.

As I began my lecture, I found it hard not to keep looking in her direction. I would have liked to dismiss everyone else and have her stay behind to read her essay out loud to me. I was dying to know her notion of what her first time would feel like and how it would change her.

And then I had to take a seat behind a desk to hide my growing erection.

If this young woman had any idea of what she did to me, she'd probably run out of the room in a panic.

Or not.

I refocused my thoughts, consciously avoiding looking in her direction. I had a lecture to deliver and while half the class probably didn't give a shit, the others looked at least marginally interested.

When it came time to collect the essays, it was tempting to just walk up and take Birdie's from her and have everyone else pile theirs on my desk for Kai to pick up, read, and grade later. But I forced myself to maintain some level of professionalism as I walked around the room gathering them.

The football corner was surprisingly occupied, but rather than having any essays to hand in, they all had the same answer for me. No surprise there. The athletic department's academic advisor was helping them finish their work, and she'd turn them in to me when they were complete.

More like she was probably writing the papers for them.

But I wasn't going to let that bother me, especially not when my fingertips grazed Birdie's as she handed me her paper. All I wanted to do was take those fingers and start kissing my way up her arm until…

I shook my head to clear my thoughts, smiled at her, and moved on.

Once I reached the front row, I wasn't shocked when the chronically late front row girls had nothing to give me.

"Are you ladies part of the football team, whose asses are covered by an academic advisor? Or do you just not give a damn about class assignments?"

They looked at me in complete surprise, unaccustomed to being called out.

And I wasn't done.

"The football players have an excuse, bullshit though it may be. It's part of the game here. We all feed at the football trough, and if they don't want to do their work, the athletic department covers for them."

One of the players in the back chuckled. They knew how the game was played as well as I did. I could be annoyed, but I was ultimately powerless.

But the other students, I had no patience for.

I scanned the room. "For those of you who didn't bother with the assignment, if you aren't interested in this class, why sign up for it?"

I turned my back on them, waving my hand. "Dismissed," I said.

I interrupted the stampede for the exit by calling Birdie aside.

Once the room was otherwise empty, she approached me. "Looks like you're having a bad day, Professor Blake."

I hung my head. "I'm sorry you had to see that. I'm

sorry the entire class had to see that. I should have kept my frustrations to myself. We all know disinterested students are part of the job. That's not going to change, no matter how much I bitch at them."

I picked up the stack of essays and rifled through them. "But there's nothing in any of these papers that particularly interests me. Except yours."

A slight blush washed over her face, and the twitching in my cock started up again.

I decided to lay it all out, and if it blew up in my face, so be it. "This entire follow-up assignment was designed with you in mind. Since I received your first essay, I've had difficulty focusing on anything besides the things you wrote. I'd like to discuss, and… *explore*, your predicament. Would you come home with me, so we can have a bit of privacy?"

15

BIRDIE JOHNSON

I LOOKED AROUND NERVOUSLY to ensure we were alone, and that this whole thing—Professor Blake's 'proposition'—wasn't some sort of a setup.

He lifted his eyebrows, smiled, and cocked his head to one side. He sat there with his ass propped on the corner of his desk while I stood just beyond arm's reach, my knees weakening in the face of his gorgeous smile.

Why did he have to be so damn good-looking?

Birdie Johnson from twenty-four hours ago would have found a reason, any reason, to say no and vanish as quickly as possible, buried in her cloak of nerdiness.

Today's Birdie Johnson, however, was emboldened by some sort of change, ready to shed labels like 'nerd' and 'geek' and 'loser' and 'virgin.'

I stood up straight, looked him in the eye, and said "Yes. Yes, please."

He stood, closing the distance between us, standing

near enough that I could feel the heat from his body. "Can I ask you for one little favor?"

I gulped. Oh god.

He placed a hand on my arm and the electricity nearly brought me to my knees. "What I'd really, really like—"

Do not faint. Do. Not. Faint.

"—is for you to call me *Cary.*"

Without meaning to, I emitted a huge sigh of relief, followed by a clumsy snort. "Right. Sorry. I keep forgetting."

Good one, Birdie.

But he either hadn't noticed, or was too polite to let on he had. Instead, he brushed the back of his hand down the side of my cheek. And without meaning to, I turned toward his fingers, finding them with my lips. My eyes fell closed. I swallowed hard. The butterflies in my stomach fluttered in a dangerous frenzy.

I looked up at him. "Sure. Cary."

Cary. The word felt good on my lips.

We started walking and soon found ourselves off campus in a quiet, leafy residential neighborhood, one I'd visited once or twice when Jessa and I had unsuccessfully tried to take up jogging.

After turning a corner, we ran into a section of cute rowhouses, and Cary led me up the steps into the fourth one.

It was funny to be in a professor's home. You knew so little about them. In the case of this one, I knew where he'd studied and gotten his PhD, what one or two of his favorite books were, and that he wore jeans every day.

And I only knew that much from his syllabus and seeing him three times a week for the past couple months. Any more than that was a complete unknown.

I looked around the sunny space, tidy in a hotel-room sort of way. I'd heard through the grapevine he'd recently gotten divorced, and I chalked up his decorating style to what Jessa would call 're-bachelorizing.' It looked kind of like he'd entered a furniture store and bought an entire model room. I suspected he wanted something modern and tasteful, which he didn't have to give any thought to. Like a lot of guys, his top priority was probably having a living room where he could kick back with a beer, prop his feet up on a coffee table, and watch the latest game.

He noticed me looking around. "I haven't lived here long. I still have some decorating to do."

There was only one framed photograph, stuck in the corner of a bookshelf. "Who are these people?"

He took the photo from me and smiled, possibly encouraged I'd gravitated to the only thing in the room that indicated a personal touch.

"My parents," he said, running a finger over the dusty glass.

He showed me into an office off the living room that had built-in bookshelves on three walls. A pile of boxes filled with books sat in one corner and the entire flat surface of the desk in the room was covered in more books.

I could relate. I didn't know what it was, but I prized books, too. All sorts of books. The more, the better.

He put his hands on his hips, looking around like he was surprised the room hadn't straightened itself up without him. "Hey, I might need somebody with library experience for this mess. Do you know anyone?"

I looked around like I was considering the job, raising an eyebrow and surprising myself with my newfound cheekiness. "I know somebody... but she doesn't come cheap."

"Well then, I'll have to check my budget. When can you start?" he said with a crooked smile.

I brought my hand to my chest in a dramatic measure. "Cary, I didn't mean me. I meant my boss at the library. She has way more experience than I do."

He laughed. "Right. Makes perfect sense. I mean, it's all about experience, isn't it? And gaining experience is what this visit is all about, beautiful girl."

Holy crap. I'd never been called *beautiful girl*. Of course it wasn't true. But it felt nice.

And it wasn't the only thing that felt nice. Before I knew it, Cary had lifted my hands toward his chest, bending to kiss me. It was a long, slow one that had me whimpering into his mouth from its intensity.

Leaning forward, he put his hands behind my knees, scooping me up into his arms. I didn't want to stop kissing him, but I had to say having him lift, hold, and carry me so effortlessly was pretty freaking cool.

He carefully took me up a narrow stairway to his bedroom, a room with large windows, and laid me down on the bed, my head resting on a pile of pillows.

My heart was pounding out of my chest, so loudly I was sure he could hear it. I couldn't believe I was here, with one of the most handsome men I'd ever laid eyes on, in his bedroom.

It was so surreal.

On hands and knees, he moved across and over me, bending low to kiss me again. My pulse jumped as his fingertips grazed the bare skin on my hip where my shirt had moved away from my jeans.

He slipped his hand up my ribcage, moving his lips from my mouth to my forehead, then to my cheeks, and down my throat.

I wanted his mouth *everywhere*.

"Mmmm," he muttered. "So beautiful, so beautiful," he said, discarding his own shirt.

I marveled at his manly chest, thick muscle covered with a light spray of masculine hair. I lifted my hands to his pecs, running them down to his abs and back up to his shoulders. God, he felt good.

He edged my shirt up until my entire middle was bare, and he lowered his face to kiss my belly. Then, for the first time in my life, a man undid the clasp on my jeans, followed by easing the zipper down and shimmying them just low enough that he could kiss across my panty line as I buried my fingers in his hair.

As he kissed me, I pulled my shirt up and off and let

it fall from the bed. He reached up and kneaded my right breast through my bra.

I gasped loudly.

With his other hand, he tugged at my jeans, wriggling them down and off and leaving me in only my bra and panties.

I urgently pulled him back up to kiss my mouth, and as he did, his leg wound up between my legs, his thigh pressing into my sex. He kissed me hungrily, grinding and rubbing against me.

My hips instinctively rose to meet his thigh as his hand slipped behind my ass, pulling me closer.

I buried my face in his chest as I shook and bucked through my panties against his leg in the first climax I'd ever shared with another person. Neither of us were even naked yet and I'd already had an orgasm.

I didn't yet have much experience, but so far? Sex was decidedly *not* awful.

It was my turn to be the aggressor, so I initiated the next round of kissing as my climax waned. As good as his thigh felt, I wanted his dick. I wanted to get *fucked.*

I reached down to unbuckle his belt, but he eased my hands away. "There's no rush, gorgeous. I need to taste you first."

"Oh, god," I said, my head rolling back and my neck arching as he slipped my panties down and off.

He reached for my left breast, drawing his fingers closed, tugging at my nipple through the lace of my bra. Electricity raced straight to my pussy, and I squirmed and moaned with embarrassing desperation.

The muscles up and down my body clenched in a confused response to all the overwhelming new sensations I was experiencing.

He kissed the insides of my thighs, pushing aside the crotch of my panties, and then ran his lips around and above my clit. Arousal seeped out of me, which I didn't even know was possible. He slowly slipped one finger inside, pushing in an upwards motion.

I arched to get something, *anything* to touch me where I so desperately needed it, but he was too strong and held me in place as I whimpered with frustration.

His tongue moved lower, where his finger explored me. He lapped, slowly and softly at first, and then fervently, his tongue replacing his finger and teasing into my entrance, tasting everything I had to offer.

I stiffened under his wicked tongue, my moans growing louder.

In response, he plunged his tongue inside me.

My legs pushed down on him, and not for a moment was I concerned with his comfort or even ability to breathe. He'd summoned forth another orgasm from me, and he would have to endure the full measure of it.

Sorry, not sorry.

I screamed and arched and thrashed as I came, a life-changing kind of climax against which my entire life might be remembered—there was everything that happened before Cary Blake, then everything that happened after.

At least that's how it seemed at the time.

When the moment began to pass, I pulled my legs closed as everything had become one giant nerve-ending. I needed a break.

He moved back up my body, his devastating smile glistening with my juices. He expertly slipped my bra off, leaving me completely naked and aware of my vulnerability in the afterglow.

As if sensing my flash of discomfort, he pulled a sheet around us as he slid next to me on the bed. We kissed deeply, and the fact that I could taste myself on his mouth sent little tremors through me.

"Your body is divine, beautiful," he said as he kissed his way around my breasts, maddeningly avoiding my nipples. "I never want to stop touching and tasting you."

Promise you never will, I wanted to say.

But I didn't.

My time there with him was a one-off, I was sure. I fought the rise of any expectations. I was no fool.

But as much as I might have wanted him to, he didn't dampen my hopes. "If it were up to me, we would never leave this bed," he said, pulling me onto my knees and getting behind me.

He continued kissing the back of my neck as he reached around to strum at my bare nipples, grazing them again and again as I gasped each time.

My pussy was an inferno, threatening to consume me. I writhed back against him, not sure what he had next in mind, but knowing what I wanted the final result to be.

"Please Cary," I begged. "I need you. I need *it*. Please."

"What do you need, Birdie? Tell me," he whispered in a naughty voice.

He wedged between my legs and when a single finger found its way inside me, I was jolted out of my haze, a landslide of explicitness pouring out of my mouth. "Fuck me, Cary, please. Fuck me with your fingers, your cock, your mouth, fuck me every way you will, all I need is for you to fuck me!"

As I screamed and begged for Cary Blake's dick, I realized maybe the sex goddess, back in the dorm, wasn't just putting on a show after all. I was coming to understand what sexual tension was all about, and if Cary's neighbors, or even anyone in a ten-block radius heard me, I couldn't have cared less.

"Beautiful, when you ask like that, how can I refuse?" he whispered into my ear.

I turned over to face him, and he kissed me once more, allowing me to fumble his belt buckle open and then his pants.

All that remained were his boxers, barely containing his erection, and when I stroked his entire length through the fabric, and it throbbed in my hand, I gasped, my own body gushing again, preparing for what was next.

16

PROFESSOR CARY BLAKE

I'D DONE EVERYTHING SLOWLY, *excruciatingly slowly*, for Birdie's benefit. I'd wanted to be inside her since the moment we'd walked through my front door, and I could wait no longer. It was time.

And as much as I loved going down on her, and as delicious as she was, my cock's patience had reached its limit.

She stroked me through my boxers, trembling when I shimmied them down, my dick springing up to hit my stomach.

"I have to fuck you, beautiful," I growled, pulling her in for another kiss as our bodies shifted and stretched, mine hovering over hers.

As soon as I'd slipped on a condom, her legs parted in surrender. I grabbed her ass, tilting her hips forward to receive me. Interlacing the fingers of one of my hands with hers, I positioned my cock at her opening, sliding it up and down and tentatively easing forward.

She gasped when my cockhead slipped inside. I could have come right there, looking into her heavy-lidded eyes and listening to her whimpers, her velvet pussy welcoming my erection. But I fought the temptation. I was going to make this last as long as Birdie wanted it.

After giving her a little more, she tensed, her knees squeezing into my sides. I let go of her hands and she threw her arms around my neck for purchase, her nails clawing me, her eyes squeezing shut.

"Am I hurting you?"

She shook her head *no,* but her slight grimace told me otherwise.

"I can stop anytime, you know. Just say the word."

She shook her head frantically. "No. Please don't stop. I want it."

"If you want it, you have to let me in," I whispered, pushing further.

Seconds later it seemed like everything inside her turned liquid. With three more mini-thrusts, I was buried to the hilt, resting as she grew accustomed to the stretch.

The struggle to hold my orgasm was monumental, especially as her pussy grabbed my cock when I began to thrust in and out.

I accelerated my pace, watching her eyes close and her teeth grit. I could have been much more aggressive, but I didn't want to be too much too soon.

What started as quiet soft moans became guttural, and her nails once again pierced the flesh of my back.

"You still good, beautiful?" I asked.

"Yeah. It does hurt," she said between ragged breaths, "but it's also so fucking good. Your cock is so fucking good."

"All right then. Good girl," I said, driving harder. "Your pussy is heavenly. Just pure heaven," I breathed into the crook of her neck.

We both knew what was coming when she began to tremble. I first felt it in her thighs.

"Tell me again," she begged. "Tell me I'm a good girl. Your good girl."

She shrieked as her orgasm arrived, racking her body with trembling spasms, her tight pussy milking my shaft so hard it almost hurt.

As she came, I tormented her with the words she'd wanted to hear. "Such a good girl, Birdie," I repeated, my own release moments away. "I can feel you coming on my dick and it feels so fucking good. I'm gonna explode in your pussy. Are you ready, my good girl?"

My last half dozen thrusts slammed into her, and our shouts and screams reached a unified crescendo.

I erupted inside Birdie's glorious body, an orgasm that seemed to never end—long, intense, and unforgettable.

As I pulled out and rolled alongside her, she put her hands between her legs, I assumed to soothe her sore flesh. I pulled her into the crook of my arms, kissing her face everywhere I could reach.

Incredible. Just incredible.

"Damn. I feel like *I* was the virgin, Birdie. Nothing

has ever felt that fucking amazing. *You're* amazing. Beautiful and amazing."

She nestled into me, my fingertips tracing up and down her back and along the curve of her hip.

"Hey. How 'bout I run you a bath?"

She nodded. "That sounds great."

Releasing her was the last thing I wanted to do, but I extricated myself and headed for the bathroom. A favorite feature of my house was an enormous, claw-footed tub, perfect for full immersion after a hard workout. I knew Birdie would love it.

When I returned to the bedroom, I found her sleeping hard, her curls haloing her head in the most perfect representation of how I felt about her. The sheets partially obscured her body, but a nipple here and a thigh there were visible, revealing just enough to return my cock to attention. But all I let myself do was stand there, watching her chest rise and fall while the water crashed into the tub behind me.

Since I'd begun teaching, I'd vowed never to get involved with a student. There were just too many ways it could go wrong, bring my career crashing to an end, and create other sorts of havoc.

And for the years I was married, it had ceased to cross my mind. But I was a single man again, and it was impossible to ignore someone like Birdie. On one hand, I thought I might regret my time with her, but I knew without a doubt if I hadn't spent the time with her I had, I'd regret *that* more than anything.

And if she'd have me, this wouldn't be a one-time thing.

Watching her, the fullness in my heart left me without regret. I had no way of knowing what the future held, and how this would affect my, or her, future at Wellshire, but I'd never felt closer to perfection than I did then.

I stopped the tub at three-quarters full, then sat on the edge of the bed. "Your bath is ready, beautiful," I whispered, kissing her shoulder.

Stretching like a cat, she sat up and swung her legs off the side of the bed.

I took her hand and helped her to the tub, and when she slid into it, she held the sides to keep from going under. "I could practically swim in here."

She closed her eyes and luxuriated, eventually letting herself sink all the way down, disappearing for a few seconds under the water before reappearing with a grin.

I felt silly standing there naked, but when I went to put on my robe hanging on the back of the bathroom door, she stopped me. "Don't you dare," she said. "I want to see you."

Returning to the edge of the tub, I watched the water swirl around her pointed nipples.

I reached for one of her hands. "How was it for you?" I asked.

She lay back and looked up at the ceiling. "It hurt a little at first, but then it was mind-blowing. I can't wait to do it again, and again, and again."

"Was it… worth the wait?" I asked.

"For a reward like that, I would have waited a thousand years," she said, smiling.

I laughed, and we both looked down where I'd propped my ass on the edge of the tub. Fuck if I wasn't already hard again.

"Touch it," she said, gesturing at my erection. "I want to watch you."

Fucking A. My kind of girl.

"You want to watch me jerk myself?" I asked, not waiting for an answer. I took my cock and without hesitation, stroked it from bottom to top.

"What if I do it, too?" she asked, and her shoulders shuddered. It wasn't lost on me that her hands had been below the water for quite some time.

"Well, fuck," I said, going at it in earnest, holding my balls in one hand as I pumped my dick with the other.

Her luscious lips closed tightly, and her nostrils flared. There was no mistaking that she was approaching another release, just like I was.

"Fuck," I growled, my balls pulling tight like they always did right before an explosion.

"Yeah. That's what I wanted. I wanted to see you jerk your cock and make yourself come. Keep going, keep coming for me," she said in a raspy voice.

After a moment, she hung her head back and shuddered from her own orgasm, her lips slightly parted, her movements causing the tub water to sway.

When we were back in bed, because there was

nowhere else we wanted to be, we held hands, grins plastered on our faces.

"Do you like Thai food?" I asked.

"Oh god, I love it. The spicier, the better," she said. "And now that you mention food, I am freaking starving."

Forty minutes later, we sat on my sofa, since I had no dining table yet, eating pad Thai and coconut chicken soup. Birdie was adorable in my robe, and I chilled in a pair of flannel PJ bottoms.

I couldn't ever recall a meal so delicious, or company so lovely. When we finished, we wound up naked in my bed again, finally falling asleep in each other's arms.

17

BIRDIE JOHNSON

I WASN'T one to miss class, but European history would have to happen without me.

By the time my eyes opened and I figured out where I was, class had already begun. Cary was still asleep, and I wondered if he, too, had somewhere he had to be that morning. But waking him would mean our little universe of two was over. That was the last thing I wanted.

Fuck, I was in trouble.

The comforter had slid from his shoulder, and as I looked at his strong jawline and muscled arms, my hand wandered to my tender pussy.

Things down there ached, but it was nothing agonizing—just a welcome reminder of the last twelve-plus hours. I felt like a different person, waking up in a world where everything was changed.

I was part of the club. And now I could see what the big fuss was about.

I also felt a little shitty for judging my dorm neighbor, sex goddess. If I had someone fucking me like Cary, well I'd be screaming my ass off, too, all the time. How could I not?

His eyelids fluttered open, and he smiled. "Hey, beautiful girl," he said, yawning and rubbing his eyes.

And damn if he wasn't rocking the cutest case of bedhead.

"Hey, yourself," I said.

Cary reached for his phone and laughed after he looked at it.

"Is everything okay?" I asked.

"I was supposed to go on a run this morning with Leo Vale and Kai. They've been trying to reach me. If they only knew." He laughed again, setting his phone down.

I hadn't spent any time considering how sleeping with Cary might impact whatever budding relationships I had with Kai or Leo. Or what it might do to their working relationships.

Had I created a huge mess?

"Oh crap," I said. "If you need to go, I get it. I've already missed a class. Guess I should have set an alarm."

"No, no, it's not like that," he insisted. "What I mean is, if they knew I was with you. It would be— well, honestly, I don't know what it would be."

"I don't want to mess up your job," I said. "I don't want you to worry about me like, 'falling in love with you' or anything silly like that."

But the truth was, I sort of was already falling for him. And Leo. And Kai.

"Birdie," he began. "I didn't bring you here to take your virginity and send you packing. Are you kidding? I have no expectations either way, but I'm keeping an open mind. You're a smart, beautiful girl and I feel strongly about you. I'd like for us to spend time together. The thing is—I'm not the only one."

"What do you mean? Not the only one *what*?"

My heart slammed in my chest. Thank god I still had the bed under me for support.

"Well—and this shouldn't really come as a surprise —my colleague, Leo Vale, for one. He thinks very highly of you. He told me he even asked you out. And Kai, my TA, told me he kissed you, so it's clear he's interested, too. If either of them had a notion that I missed a workout because I was in bed with the object of their affection—well, I think they'd be totally psyched for me."

What?

My head was swimming. All my life I'd been ignored by guys, written off time and again for one reason or another. Now, all of a sudden, like the universe was making up for lost time or maybe atoning for its guilt in denying me, three men, three *men*, were interested in me? And not just interested, but *interested*?

Bizarre didn't begin to describe it.

Under normal circumstances, I'd have been over-joyed to have any of the three of these guys glance in my direction. But *this*? What the hell did I do with *this*?

Cary propped himself up on an elbow and looked at me. "I think I want some breakfast," he said with a mischievous grin.

"What do you have in mind?" I asked, realizing my stomach was growling. The Thai delivery we'd enjoyed the night before seemed like days ago.

But food turned out not to be an immediate concern. "Well, all that's on my mind is you," Cary said, disappearing under the covers.

In moments, his mouth was on my pussy, lapping me from ass to clit and back, and my mind was no longer puzzling over any juggling act involving three men. There was no pretense on Cary's part. He dove in with passion, abandoning his slow approach from the day before. His tongue swirled on my clit, and I came in a flood, my hands on the back of his head, urging him to take me to heaven again.

After a second round of his mouth bringing me another glorious orgasm, I begged off the idea of continuing. The truth was, I was sore. I needed a break.

I was afraid he'd be disappointed, but he kissed me, saying the pleasure was his.

Not sure the pleasure was *all* his, but I wasn't going to argue.

He scrolled through his phone to make some 'adjustments' to his schedule given his late morning, and excused himself for the bathroom.

As I lay there looking at my own phone, I thought I heard a noise downstairs. But I chalked it up to being in a new place. Cary's bed was so comfortable and my body so relaxed it would have taken a tank driving through the front door to get me up and off my ass.

Or so I thought.

I turned to lay my phone down on the nightstand when something bumped the bed. Scared shitless, I whipped around and was greeted by a tongue. Not Cary's, but a dog's. A pug's, to be exact, standing on his hind legs to check me out, breathing loudly and shaking his butt to say hello.

He licked my face, and I sat up to get my bearings. "Hello there," I said. "Where did you come from?" He spun in circles, let out a little bark in reply, and jumped up to join me on the bed, where I read his tag and found out his name was Wilbur.

Cary emerged from the bathroom and turned white as a sheet. "Oh, shit," he said. "Um, I'll be right back." He grabbed a pair of pajama pants from the dresser and rushed out the door.

Wilbur stayed on the bed with me, rolling on his back to have his tummy rubbed.

"What were you thinking?" Cary shouted angrily from downstairs. "You can't just barge in here."

Oh crap. What was going on?

"You knew I was dropping the dog off," a woman said coldly. There was something vaguely familiar about her voice, but I couldn't place it.

I strained my ears but only caught snippets of a hellacious argument taking place either in Cary's kitchen or living room.

"I bet she's still upstairs!" the woman roared.

Oh my god. Was there someone else? Or was I the someone else? I silently slipped out of bed and began to pull my jeans back on.

"Who are you even talking about?" Cary yelled, clearly exasperated.

Wilbur looked up at me for reassurance, and I gave him the same look back.

"You didn't even bother to hide her shoes!"

"This is *my* house. I don't have to hide anything! If I have a guest over, that's none of your goddamn business! Do not come in my house again without being invited first, do you hear me?"

"Asshole!" was the last thing I heard, followed by the front door slamming.

Cary flew back upstairs. "Sorry about that, Birdie," he said. "It was my ex-wife. Not the most harmonious separation, I'm afraid."

Right. The ex-wife.

How many people had their exes just walk into their house whenever they wanted?

"I guess she… has her own key?" I asked quietly.

He nodded, scratching Wilbur behind the ears. I wasn't sure if he was comforting himself, or the dog.

"She does, so she can get Wilbur when I'm not home. But I'm beginning to think that's not such a great idea."

"Does… does this happen a lot? Your wife walking in on… female company?" I asked, afraid of the answer I might get.

His head whipped in my direction. "No. It's actually

never happened. I think that's why she was so taken aback. I... since our split, I haven't had another woman to my home. I haven't even been with another woman."

Wow.

I finished dressing and walked over to the edge of the bed where he sat. I ran my fingers through his bed head hair and along his beautiful jawline. "Wilbur didn't like the fighting. He was shaking."

Cary picked up the dog and held him tight. "He's a nervous little guy. Thank you for taking care of him."

"He's very sweet. Very friendly."

Cary looked up from Wilbur. "It's interesting, He's usually wary of strangers, but he warmed right up to you."

"He clearly has excellent taste." I laughed.

"You have no idea how excellent you taste," Cary replied, his eyes twinkling.

Oh god. If we got things started up again, we'd never see the light of day.

"I wish there was time for you to taste me some more," I said. "But even though I didn't mind missing one class today, I have another I have to get to. Sorry!"

"Don't apologize. I'm with ya on that. I gotta get my ass over to campus, too."

He set Wilbur down and walked over.

Holding my shoulders, he looked down at me. "I hope you understand, but this wasn't some sort of one-time thing. At least not for me. I don't know exactly what it *is*, but I'm open to exploring it if you are."

I kissed him deeply, and his cock grew, pressing against me through the material of his pants.

"If you don't get dressed right this instant, I'm going to have to fuck you again," Cary said, grabbing handfuls of my ass and grinding me against his bulge. I threw my hands behind his neck, my hips rolling against him.

"Damn!" he moaned when I broke the kiss off.

"We have to go. C'mon," I said, throwing his clothes at him.

I never thought I'd be pestering a professor to get his ass in gear for school.

But, there we were.

After half-walking, half-running to my psych study, I arrived just in time. The ever-cranky Professor Judge rolled her eyes at me as I took my seat.

Jesus, lady. This wasn't a damn job.

But I was required to take part, so I was eager to get things over with.

She looked around the room of about fifteen people from my larger psych class. "We'll open with two short films and then you'll fill out anonymous surveys based on your own sexual experiences," she explained. The lights dimmed, and the videos began.

The first dealt with expectations versus experiences, from male and female perspectives, of first sexual experiences.

There were gay and straight and group experiences, and throughout the interviews a couple of trends became clear—the guys expected their first times to be great and they overwhelmingly reported that their expectations were met or exceeded. The women reported being more leery and more hesitant, and it turned out they had good reason to be.

I was not even twenty-four hours removed from losing my virginity, and I felt a little guilty that it had been so mind-blowingly good when so many of the women in the interviews reported the opposite.

I had hoped that my conversation with Jess and Roxy about an experienced man being better in bed might bear fruit, but I hadn't realized how right they were until I heard interview after interview describing brief, uncomfortable encounters, and then being abandoned in the aftermath.

Cary had been nothing like that.

The second video was also filled with interviews of men and women, but rather than discussing first times, they talked about their sex lives as a whole—what they expected, what the reality was like, and what they hoped they might experience in the future.

Fascinating.

What became quickly apparent was a disconnect called the 'orgasm gap.' A significant percentage of the women reported that they never achieved orgasm with a partner, while nearly all the men claimed their female partners did.

The room was full of snickers, the women holding their heads high at being validated, and the guys looking around sheepishly.

The more I learned about what was really happening in people's bedrooms, the luckier I realized I was. And the more I thought about it, and about Cary Blake's mouth and hands and cock, the hornier I got.

By the time the second movie ended, I needed a fan to calm myself down, or at least make a run for the nearest bathroom to relieve myself.

But before I could take action, we were given a link for filling out a questionnaire.

Names weren't asked for, of course, but dates, ages, and circumstances were, in a survey about our own first and most recent sexual encounters.

I answered honestly, sharing that my most recent was *also* my first, chuckling to myself that I was probably the only person in the history of the study to have arrived, basically, directly from her first time.

By the time class let out, I was simmering inside, aching for more of Cary. I headed for his office, hopeful that I might be able to convince him to indulge me in a quick midday tryst.

18

KAI FLEMINSTER

THE STACK of essays was mind-numbing. I went through it twice searching for Birdie's, but it was nowhere to be found.

I stuck a pin in my imaginary Professor Blake voodoo doll. *That'll teach him to keep the good stuff for himself!*

Red pen in hand, I went through two essays and feared I'd run out of ink long before getting through the entire stack, and that was just noting grammatical errors.

I got up and stretched, then looked out the window to see if I could spot the coffee cart outside anywhere. I slipped my flip flops back on, grabbed my keys and phone, and headed out to see if it was on the other side of the building.

Exiting the office, I rounded the nearest corner and almost crashed into a student.

No fucking way. It was Birdie.

"We've got to stop meeting like this." I laughed, catching her before she went down, that's how hard we'd collided.

"Kai," she said, "I was just on my way to your office."

Damn that smile of hers.

I barely resisted the urge to bend down and kiss her. "Well, I was stepping out for coffee. I'm grading your class's essays, but they were so boring I was afraid I might doze off."

She looked horrified, and I realized I needed to keep my mouth shut. A teacher didn't need to say things like that to a student.

"Was mine that bad?" she asked, grimacing.

I could see she was concerned about her paper, but there was also something else going on for her.

Had she….?

"I hate to tell you, Johnson, but your essay was the worst," I teased. "Just dreadful. You didn't take any of the advice I offered. You'll have to do some pretty serious convincing to get me to change your grade to passing. Want to head back to the office to discuss it?"

She hopped from one foot to the other, like she wanted to race me there. "Well, if it's the only chance to rescue my essay, how can I say no?"

Coffee forgotten, we headed for the office.

"Miss Johnson, do you have an explanation for this?" I asked, waving around a blank piece of paper in mock anger.

She hung her head dutifully, trying not to laugh. "I tried what you suggested. But what happened instead was that I got caught by Professor Vale watching YouPorn in the library, lost my earbuds in the process, blasted the sounds of sex from my phone as I ran through the library to get away, and then burst into tears in front of him for being such a loser. So, things didn't work out too great."

"Are you… is that really what happened?" I asked, also trying not to laugh.

She nodded slowly. "Pretty much."

I placed both my balled-up hands near my head and opened them as if my head had just exploded. "Tell. Me. Everything."

She recounted watching YouPorn in a quiet study room, and nearly having a coronary when Vale popped into the room. She fell out of her chair, losing her earbuds, which disconnected Bluetooth, leaving the audio to play at full blast through her phone speaker.

It was like a scene out of a hilarious movie.

And it also had me rock hard.

The thought of her getting all worked up in the library and then broadcasting what she was watching to everyone was just too much, especially since it was unintentional and so embarrassing. I wouldn't have wished that on my worst enemy.

But that didn't mean I didn't think it was funny as hell.

Since we were in the midst of some sort of role play, and she seemed to be even more into it than I was, I decided to do something reckless. To be more accurate, my hard cock decided my mouth should do something reckless.

"Since this essay doesn't demonstrate a firm grasp of the material, maybe it would be better if you demonstrated what you learned, Miss Johnson," I said sternly.

She blushed red and looked down at her shoes.

Shit. Had I overplayed my hand?

If she took what I said to the administration, even if I claimed it was in jest, my dreams of becoming a professor were over. My father and grandfather were right—messing around with students was a road to ruin.

But at that moment, my little head was doing all my thinking, and I reasoned that any chance to hook up with a girl like Birdie was worth the risk.

Her gaze rose to meet mine. "I... I can do that," she said bashfully.

She circled the desk and straddled my lap. We kissed hungrily, and she was even more delicious than I remembered. She smelled oddly like men's body wash. It wasn't a bad smell, just unexpected.

Regardless, my dick throbbed uncomfortably in my pants beneath her, and as we kissed, I tried to sneak a hand to adjust myself.

To my surprise, Birdie got there first.

"Oh!" she exclaimed at my hardness.

She slid off me and to her knees. "Let me show you what I learned from the videos," she said looking up at me.

Unbuckling my pants, I pushed them to my ankles.

Since I was going commando, my erection sprung free, waving in the air in front of Birdie's beautiful face.

She took my shaft in both hands, wrapping her fingers around it and starting with a slow pumping motion. Maintaining eye contact the entire time, she pulled it forward, taking the head into her mouth.

I groaned with pleasure as she kissed and licked me, her passion making up for any lack of experience or technique.

For the first time, I doubted Birdie's claim of virginity. Nobody so eager to suck cock could possibly be new to it. Those thoughts, however, quickly vanished in a haze of bliss. Her plump lips, so perfect for kissing, were even better at what she was doing now.

I lost my hands in her hair, pulling her closer and urging her to take me deeper.

"Goddamn, baby," I gasped, her tongue swirling lewdly around my cock, bringing me closer and closer to coming.

I reached for her, pulling her away from my dick to bring her back up to kiss me. She was voracious, her tongue in my mouth, wild with lust. As we kissed, she reached down to continue stroking my cock.

With her free hand, she reached for the buckle of her jeans, which I helped her shed along with her panties. She climbed back onto my lap, giving me a moment to sheath myself with a condom. She then impaled herself on my dick, sliding down to take my full length all at once. I gritted my teeth with the effort it took to contain myself, wanting to prolong this unexpected encounter as long as possible.

She remained completely filled with me, rocking her hips as our lips mashed each other's. Any doubt I had about her being or not being a virgin prior to this moment no longer mattered.

I placed my hands on her hips to bounce her up and down. She locked eyes with me, hers filled with fire.

The position was just too good, and I knew I couldn't last long without something to focus on besides how incredible Birdie's wet pussy was.

I pulled her shirt up and off and tossed it onto the desk. She responded by removing her bra, leaving her naked. And mouth-watering.

I sought her swollen nipples, grazing them with my teeth and sucking them hard and deep. She groaned, bouncing harder and faster on my cock.

"I'm so close, I'm gonna come so hard," she managed through great gasps of air.

"Do it, Birdie, let me feel you come. Come for me," I said in a rasping voice.

Just as she started to shriek, a movement caught my eye.

Birdie continued to bounce on my dick, oblivious to the world around her.

But I looked toward the doorway, and who stood there but Professor Vale.

19

PROFESSOR LEO VALE

My second class of the day wore me down. A pretty mediocre student of mine had picked that class to argue about punctuation rules.

Not that I didn't like a debate. It was an opportunity to teach. Which was, after all, my job.

As a pick me up, I'd thought about looking for the coffee cart, partially for a cup and partially because I'd hoped to bump into Birdie again, or at least nose around for her whereabouts, if it were staffed by her roommate.

I hadn't been able to get the image of her all but masturbating in the library out of my mind, and I'd enjoyed a vivid fantasy of walking in on her in that state, closing the door, and fucking her right there on the table, audience be damned.

Of course, that would never happen.

Never.

When I wasn't able to find the wandering coffee

cart, my mood sank even further, and when I arrived at my office, I had to juggle papers, books, and my laptop bag while fumbling with the door lock. I dropped half my crap but finally got the key to turn when I heard voices from inside the office. At first, I thought it was Cary arguing with a student, and I was ready to join in, just to release the residual frustration I had from my own problem pupil. It soon became apparent, however, that what I was listening to was far from an argument.

Somebody was having sex in my office, and not quietly. I knew already from how far the knob had turned that nobody had bothered to lock the door, which made me think it was probably Kai. Cary would never have been so careless. I scanned the length of the hall, and nobody was headed in my direction.

I weighed my options. It seemed inevitable that somebody walking by would hear the parties involved sooner or later, which would be potentially disastrous. Similarly, with the door unlocked, chances were too great some student might walk in, and there, again, disaster loomed. I could stand sentry outside until they finished, but damn it, it was my office.

The voyeur in me couldn't stand the curiosity any longer, and my dick was reacting to what I was hearing, so I opened the door as quietly as possible.

What I discovered was the last thing I could have imagined, but it was at the same time blindingly hot.

A naked Birdie Johnson was straddling our TA, Kai, riding him like she was born to do it.

"I'm s... so close, I'm gonna come s... so hard," she managed to stammer.

Someone was no longer a virgin.

She was turned away from me and had no idea I was there, but no sooner had her climax begun than Kai spotted me.

His face was a mask of confusion, fear, and unmitigated lust as Birdie's sexy body writhed and came on his cock. I raised a finger to my lips to shush him lest he interrupt her orgasm, which was the sexiest fucking thing I'd ever seen.

I grabbed my cock through my pants and stroked myself as she enjoyed every delightful moment of her climax. I recalled my brief glimpse of the porn she'd been watching, which included two men and one woman. It had been years since I'd taken any psych classes, but I made the leap in my mind that if she was watching it, then it must have been something that interested her, and that I might join in. I'd never shared a woman with another man, but Kai was a cool guy, and I had to admit I was smitten with Birdie. At worst, I'd bring their party to an awkward halt. At best, I'd have a chance to give her an electrifying orgasm like the one she'd just enjoyed with Kai.

I silently slipped into the office, closing and locking the door behind me and stripping out of my clothes. My cock jutted out in front of me, and I circled the desk, coming up on Birdie's blindside just as she'd begun to slowly ride Kai again.

"I've never seen anything sexier than watching you

come, Birdie," I said as I placed my hand on the small of her back, feeling her muscles tense and relax.

She shrieked, her eyes flying wide open, terror filling them. She stiffened, looking up at me and then back at Kai. He nodded to her, holding her ass and fucking her at a steady rhythm.

Fortunately, her fear was short-lived, overcome by her sheer, wanton lust, as she realized there was not going to be any problem. At least not on my part.

She smiled at me, licked her lips, and reached for my dick, guiding it into her mouth as she continued to bounce on Kai's cock.

She was a quick study.

Her juicy lips felt even better than my wildest fantasies, gliding up and down my throbbing hardness. Kai rolled and squeezed her nipples, and she took me deeper, nearly into her throat, overcome with a hunger to please.

"She's so fucking tight," Kai groaned.

"Don't come yet," I said. "I'm your boss, I get to fuck her and come in her before you do."

She made a squealing sound and shook all over, the depravity of the situation too much for her.

"When she comes, it's like she has a hand inside her squeezing my cock. Holy fuck," Kai growled.

I could wait no longer, and lifted her up and off him and laid her across Cary's desk, pushing aside papers and a cup of pens. I rolled on a condom, then pulled her hips to the edge of the desk, watching my cock disappear inside her soaked pussy.

"Yes, fuck me," she howled.

I built up an aggressive pace, pulling her legs together and straight up against my chest. I no longer cared if somebody walking by heard us. I pounded her pussy, sexy moans erupting from deep in her throat.

Kai circled the desk. He lined up his dick with Birdie's mouth, sliding his wide head in as he cradled her face in his hands.

"Do you want this, Birdie?" I asked.

She nodded as frantically as she was able, considering she had a large cock in her mouth.

"Do you love it?"

Another nod.

"Do you *need* it?

She answered with a choking, "Mmmmm!" as she began to climax again, and I responded to the way her pussy gripped my dick by pistoning harder and deeper.

Kai went next, gasping rapid-fire and flushing from his neck up and across his face as he emptied himself into her mouth.

He staggered away and collapsed back into a chair, his chest heaving as he watched us. I started going long and slow, having spread Birdie's legs wide so I could watch her take my dick.

"Please," she said, "it hurts—so good, but it hurts—I can't take much more," she whimpered.

"This will make for quite an essay," I said, increasing my pace as my orgasm drew near.

"C-Cary fucked m-me last night," she managed to blurt as she gritted her teeth, and I fucked her harder.

"Did you know?" I asked Kai, who shook his head.

What about that was so fucking hot?

I kept pistoning our girl, reaching down to touch her face. "Did he finish inside you?" I asked.

She nodded and whimpered, and I sensed that we were close to reaching the point of losing her. She had gone from never having had a sip of beer to doing shots all night. She could take no more.

Bringing her legs back together, I went slowly, nearly all the way out, then all the way back in, and by the fourth thrust, I exploded.

Once I was finished, I helped her off the desk and onto my lap, where I'd sat in a chair. Kai's mouth covered the tops of her thighs with kisses, gently coaxing her legs apart. I thought he might try to fuck her again, but he surprised me by moving his kisses right to her overheated sex. He lapped at her freshly-fucked pussy until she was again gasping.

Eventually, he zeroed in on her clit, focusing his tongue on it until she eased him away. She was a limp ragdoll in my arms, barely coherent.

She nodded off right there, and Kai reached for a jacket hanging on the back of our office door, covering her with it.

"I'll stay here with her," I offered. "You take the rest of the day off, go get a shower and something to eat. We'll be fine"

He gave Birdie a kiss on the forehead as he left.

When she finally stirred, she bolted off my lap and looked at the time.

"Shit. I have a class in ten minutes."

She began to pull on her clothes, and I joined her since I had my own class coming up. We walked out of the office together, and before we went our separate ways, found the coffee cart. Armed with caffeine, we were as ready as we'd ever be to face the rest of our day.

Cary and I had a potentially uncomfortable conversation ahead of us, but I regretted nothing. I knew he had feelings for her, as did Kai, and now all three of us had been with her. What did that mean for the future? I had no idea.

20

BIRDIE JOHNSON

After Professor Vale treated me to a coffee, I bolted across campus, hoping I wasn't walking funny.

I sat through my next class, my pen poised on my notebook. But at the end of the fifty-minute lecture, I realized I'd written nothing but a couple scribbles. My mind was mush.

I hustled back to the dorm, praying I didn't run into anyone I knew. I was in no shape for small talk. I was actually in no shape for anything except for the long, hot shower I took when I got back, and falling into bed in my comfiest PJ bottoms and tank top.

The next day was a Saturday, so I set my alarm to wake up just early enough to call in sick at the library and arrange to take the weekend off before going right back to sleep.

Mercifully, Jessa let me sleep—far longer than was normal for me—and when I was finally ready to wake up, she had dining hall pizza, Extra Strength Tylenol, and Gatorade waiting for me. It was her tried and true hangover cure, and she figured I needed it.

Every muscle in my body ached, but it wasn't from a hangover. But I'd explain that to her when I was ready.

I hadn't heard from any of the three guys, save an email from Cary asking how I was feeling, physically and emotionally. I'd have been lying if I didn't admit my heart took a little leap when he confessed he couldn't wait to see me again next week, both in and out of class.

My head—and heart—kept going back and forth among the three of them, wondering if Kai and Leo had discussed what we'd done with Cary, and if the two of them were actually okay with what had happened between us. I worried that issues like jealousy would inevitably crop up, which would totally suck, not to mention probably put an end to any of the fun we were having.

When Monday morning arrived, my soreness was just a memory, and I looked forward to getting back on track. I hated missing class and work, but I supposed that even the nerdy but ex-virgin Birdie Johnson needed a break every now and then.

Aside from seeing Cary at the front of the room being the sexy teacher that he was, the class I was most looking forward to was psychology. What had Professor Judge done with the results of the sex study? What would I be learning about myself and about sex in general? I was like a sponge, wanting to lap up all the new knowledge I could.

Hey, I could be a sex goddess, too.

I was on time for a change, and the fact that the entire class was devoted to sex ensured everyone's full attention. It was funny to me that only a few days ago, such a class would have seemed silly and over the top, but now I was completely invested and interested and no longer the fish out of water I had been. I glanced around the large assembly of my peers and wondered how many of them had slept with a professor—and how many of them had been in threesomes. I was sad for the girls in the group who were victims of the 'orgasm gap,' and was grateful I wasn't one of them.

All the talk about sex and orgasms had me squirming by the end of class. Could I track down Cary or Leo or Kai or some combination of them to scratch my itch?

There were cute guys in the class, no doubt. I found myself checking them out, but no way saw them as potential sex partners. I was spoiled for *men*, not college boys. And even though Kai was only a few years older than most of them, there was a maturity to him that put him closer to Cary and Leo than the fraternity dudes snickering at the professor's lecture.

Once we were dismissed, the usual stampede bolted for the classroom door.

But before I got far, Professor Judge stopped me. "Birdie? Miss Johnson?" she called after me.

I turned back, honestly surprised she even knew my

name. It was a large lecture hall class, and we'd never had any sort of one-on-one interaction.

"Yes?" I said, fighting like a salmon swimming upstream to get through the exiting herd.

I had no idea why she singled me out from the group, but since I couldn't think of any negatives, aside from my occasional tardiness, I wasn't worried.

Once the room cleared, the professor walked over and sat down at the lecture hall's large desk. I stood in front of it awkwardly, not having been offered a seat. I shifted my weight from side to side as she sipped from her tumbler, looking at something on her laptop.

I didn't have all day, lady.

After what seemed like an eternity, she looked up at me.

"So. You should know, I went by my husband's place the other morning."

"Okay?" I said in a questioning tone.

How did this pertain to me?

She shook her head, chuckling. "Unbelievable. You don't know who my husband is, do you?"

"Mr. Judge, I assume?"

She pressed her lips together like she'd sucked a lemon. "No," she said curtly. "Not mister. Professor. Professor Cary Blake."

Huh?

I placed a couple fingers on the desk to retain my balance while a wave of dizziness bulldozed over me, churning my stomach acid and causing a terrible taste in my mouth.

Holy. Fucking. Shit.

Cary was her husband?

"Professor Blake?" I said in a squeaking voice.

Her face was covered with smugness. "Yes. You remember him, right? The one you were fucking the other day?"

She was the one who'd brought over the dog?

Why hadn't I just stayed in bed this morning? Like for the rest of my life?

My mind spun as I tried to get a handle on things. *How the hell did she know? And they're married? What the fuck? He said she was his ex.*

She opened her laptop again, and hit some keys to bring up my survey responses. She read through them slowly. "You really expect me to believe it was your first time, you little tramp?"

"I'm still not sure why you think… and besides, that was supposed to be anonymous—"

She cut me off. "Between this," she waved her hand at the laptop screen, "and the fact that you're wearing the same backpack and shoes that were right by the front door when I stopped by with our dog, there's no use denying it, is there, Birdie?"

I swallowed hard. "Yes, I was at his house. And he referred to you as the ex. As in, you're no longer married."

"Of course, he did," she laughed. "He probably thinks we're divorced. But I haven't signed the papers yet, so technically, we're," she held up her ring finger to show me a gold band, "still married."

Waves of nausea roiled me. Was Leo married, too? What about Kai? *Was this all just a game to them?* 'Deflower the virgin?' *How many other girls had Professor Blake done this to?*

And how was the professor able to identify my survey responses? They were private. My name was nowhere on them.

Oh god. How naïve was I, trusting everyone around me?

I should have known better. Should have known not to trust the survey, or him. What I thought had been this beautiful, shared sexual awakening was just garbage. I'd been made a fool of, and I might as well have hooked up with one of the guys stumbling back drunk from a party on Friday night puking in the trash cans outside the dorm. It would somehow be less demeaning.

My sadness turned to rage. But I didn't let on. My grades were on the line.

"I didn't know. I didn't know he was still married."

She tossed her head back and laughed. "Be that as it may, it doesn't fix anything, does it? Sorry is just a word. Stay the hell away from him or face the consequences. He'll lose his job, tenure or not, and you'll at the very least lose your scholarship, but probably also be kicked out of school. Don't test me."

I was reeling. That was the only way to describe it. I didn't know what to say or do. Everything that had been so perfect was shattered. If the ground swallowed me up at that moment, I would have been fine with it.

"Did he use protection?" she asked.

"That's private," I managed. She didn't need to know any details.

"I'll take that as a no. Oh my god, this is rich. I hadn't even considered the possibility he might have knocked you up. Good lord."

I was about to tell her we'd used condoms but couldn't really see how that information would make anything any better.

She shook her head and sighed before clicking away on her laptop. A minute passed, and I had no idea what to do or say.

"Oh, are you still here?" she sneered, glancing up at me before returning to her work. "You're dismissed."

I bolted from the lecture hall and the building, stumbling my way across campus, sure that everyone knew what a pathetic loser I was. Any thoughts I had of stopping by the guys' office were now gone. I didn't know one hundred percent that the whole thing was a setup between Cary, Leo, and Kai, but I was leaning in that direction.

Everything I had been so sure of twenty minutes ago was completely topsy-turvy. I went back to my room and screamed into my pillow until it was time to go to work. I actually couldn't wait. The library was predictable. Orderly. Calm.

Unlike every other aspect of my life.

21

PROFESSOR LEO VALE

I HADN'T SEEN Birdie since we'd gotten our coffees, and it seemed like it had been ages. I missed her. I really did.

It was so strange. Here was someone I barely knew, who was on my mind nearly round the clock. I needed to see her. How hard could she be to find?

When I was finished with my office hours, having been visited by not one but three students worried about failing my class, I headed for the library, hoping I might catch her there.

I lingered by the information desk for a moment, but when I didn't see her, took a walk upstairs.

Bingo.

I spotted her at the far end of the floor, pushing a cart filled with books.

Checking to make sure nobody else was around, I approached her in the stacks with a grin on my face and my arms spread wide. "Hello darlin', I've missed you."

However, instead of accepting my hug, or even returning my smile, she made a sour face. "What do you want?" she snapped.

To say I was floored would be an understatement. "Wh-what?" I sputtered. "What's wrong, Birdie?"

"Like I said, what do you want?" she said flatly. She returned to stocking the shelves with books, not even looking at me.

"Okay. What the hell is up?" I asked.

She shook her head and rolled the cart a few feet over to shelve more books. "Nothing. I'm working. Can you just go?"

"No, Birdie, I'm sorry, I will not. Something has clearly happened. Something is wrong, and I deserve some sort of explanation."

With a dramatic sigh, she stopped working and looked up at the ceiling, her curls falling away from her face. I thought she might burst into tears.

I stepped forward and touched her shoulder. "Birdie, I… want to make sure you're okay. If you really want me to go, I'll go, but if something's wrong, if there's any way I can help, please let me."

She looked me in the eye, searching, and finally nodded. "I want you to answer one question, and then maybe we can talk."

"Anything," I said.

"What we did—in your office—was that planned? Is this all some sort of game?"

To say I was caught off-guard wouldn't begin to describe my surprise.

"Birdie, I don't know what's prompting this, but not only no, hell no. If I've done anything to make you doubt that, let me prove myself to you."

Anger flashed in her eyes, but she considered my words. After a few moments, she nodded and asked me to follow her.

She led me to a study room, just like the one I'd found her watching porn in, and closed the door behind us. "I thought about using a storage room, but that would raise too many questions if we were discovered. In here, we'll have privacy but also plausible deniability, since I'm an English major and you're an English professor, and we're just talking about a class. While I'm supposed to be working. But whatever."

She drummed on the table with her fingers while trying to decide how to begin. "Okay. I have Professor Judge for psychology. And it seems she's married to—

"Cary," I interrupted. "Or rather, she used to be. Did she… say something to you?"

"You know her?" I asked.

"Of course. Cary is a good friend. I've known Professor Judge—I mean Joan—for years."

She narrowed her eyes at me.

What the hell had Joan done?

I knew from Cary that even though she'd initiated the divorce, Joan had gone back to him, hoping for a reconciliation. It was when he turned her down that things had started getting ugly.

"She told me I fucked her husband and that she would ruin him and me both, if I went near him again."

"Well, they're separated," I explained. "All but divorced. In fact, it's Joan who has the paperwork. All she has to do is sign, and it's official. She's torturing him over it in some sort of last minute powerplay. But regardless, Cary thinks of her as his ex."

Guess Joan hadn't reached that stage yet. But threatening Birdie? And how did she know about her, anyway?

"Do they have kids?" Birdie asked.

"No. Just a little dog. He gave her the car. He moved out. He's done everything for a clean break."

Birdie rested her chin on her hands and considered my words.

"Why are they getting divorced?"

"When they got married, they agreed no kids. She changed her mind, but he didn't. She also used to accuse him of sleeping with students, which he never did."

"Until now."

"Until now, yes. But you must understand, having done everything he could to get himself divorced, and having been separated for some time now, he considers himself single. He didn't sleep with you as some way of getting back at Joan or to sow his wild oats or some such nonsense. He cares about you. Like I do, and like Kai does."

Birdie buried her face in her hands. "What a mess. What a huge, freaking mess."

"Joan should keep her nose out of other peoples' business," I said.

"I want to believe you."

I reached across the table and took her hands in mine, not caring who might walk by and see. "You *can*," I insisted. "You should. Joan Judge doesn't get to call the shots for Cary, not anymore, and she should have no say in your life except as it pertains to her class. Let me handle her. Let me fix this. Please."

Unless I was mistaken, relief was written across Birdie's beautiful features. She nodded.

I lifted her hands and kissed them. "Trust me. I'll straighten this shit right out."

"Thank you, Leo. And sorry for biting your head off back there. I'm sure you can imagine what I was thinking after the dressing down from Professor Judge. I might be facing my first failing grade, ever."

"Not if I have anything to say about it," I said.

Leaving the library, I debated confronting Joan or talking to Cary first.

Fearing my anger might get the better of me and cause me to say things I might regret if I were face to face with Joan, I called Cary and told him I was coming over for an urgent conversation.

On the way, I stopped and grabbed a six pack.

"Hey, man, come in. What's going on? Is everything okay?" Cary asked, leading me to his kitchen.

I popped the top off two bottles.

"It's about Birdie. And Joan."

"*Joan?*"

His face paled.

I took a long pull on my beer. "Yeah. She knows you had sex with Birdie."

Cary went to say something, but I raised my hand to stop him.

"Yes, I know you did, too. And before we go any further, you should know that I also had sex with her. With Kai."

Cary laughed. "Yeah, yeah, of course you did."

"Seriously, Cary," I said. "How do you think I know that you slept with her? She told me."

He let out a long breath. "I'm going to need something stronger than this," he said, holding up his beer bottle.

"Let me start from the beginning, with what I know. Birdie came into the office looking for you the other day. Kai was there, and one thing led to another."

Cary finished his first beer and quickly drank half of his next one as I spoke.

"I walked in in the middle of it. She was on top of him, about to come. It was so—you know how beautiful she is. It was hot. And the next thing I knew, we're having a threesome."

Cary reached for a third bottle, having finished his second.

"Slow down, there, big fella," I said. "As we finished, she confessed to us about the two of you, and I admit, I wasn't proud of myself. I couldn't change what happened, although I wished I could. If I'd have known,

I never would have touched her. But I did, and it was amazing."

This time I didn't stop him from starting on his third beer, I only hoped he wouldn't smash it over my head.

"How does Joan fit into all of this?" Cary asked.

"She somehow figured out Birdie had been here, and that the two of you had hooked up. And, Birdie is in one of her classes. Joan made her feel like the two of you were still together, that she was a homewrecker, having sex with a married man. She threatened to have Birdie kicked out of school if she didn't stay away from you. She also threatened to expose you."

"What a miserable woman," Cary said angrily. He stood up and began to pace. "She came over the other morning to drop off Wilbur. Birdie was here. She must have seen her things and put the pieces together. Jesus."

"I was prepared to go right over to Joan's and confront her personally. But I didn't want to step on your toes," I said.

"Thanks," Cary replied. "I know how to deal with her. I save receipts, so to speak, and I have a doozy I've been holding on to until the time was right."

"Oh? What's that all about?"

"You'll know soon enough. But as confident as I am that I can handle Joan, what do we do about Birdie?"

"That's—*tricky*," I said. "I have no fucking idea. I don't feel right competing against you for her, but I also don't want to give her up."

He nodded. "And unless I miss my guess, Kai is pretty attached to her, too."

"Seems like he is. How does this end with nobody getting hurt? I don't see a solution besides all in or all out."

"What do you mean?" he asked.

"I mean, unless Birdie has a strong preference, which we'd all respect, of course, then we either all get involved with her, or we all politely distance ourselves."

"How the hell would that work?" Cary asked. "How can all three of us be 'involved' with her?"

"Have you ever met a woman who felt like she was getting enough of your attention?" I asked. "There aren't enough hours in the day, especially in our line of work, am I right? With three of us, we could fulfill all of her emotional and intellectual needs. And sexually? She's a dynamo. I'm not even sure the three of us can keep up."

"Did you go down on her?" Cary asked.

"I didn't get the chance."

"Well, I think I'm addicted," he said with a laugh.

"I feel the same way about her mouth," I said. "Not sure where that leaves Kai, though."

We both laughed.

"If he's getting to fuck Birdie Johnson, it leaves him ecstatic," Cary said.

We headed out, me in the direction of home, and Cary in the direction of his ex.

2 2

BIRDIE JOHNSON

I STOPPED outside the psychology building and summoned my nerve. A shot of liquor would have been nice, but positive self-talk would have to do.

Leo had urged me to trust him, and save for a brief text conversation with Kai, I'd been incommunicado. I skipped Cary's class, still not sure I could face him until the business with Professor Judge had been resolved.

You can do this, Birdie, I said to myself. *You're a badass and she sucks and you're in the right.* I was only slightly convinced.

Joan Judge had so thoroughly crushed and humiliated me the last time I'd faced her that I'd rather have gone to the dentist for a quadruple root canal than put myself at her mercy again.

All that inspired me to put one foot in front of the other and walk down the hallway was Leo's confidence in me. Cary's smile. Kai's ability to make me laugh. I had feelings for all of them, despite the tumultuous past forty-eight hours, and if I wanted to get over this hurdle and back to the delightful uncertainty of my three sexy suitors, I had to face Joan Judge woman to woman, on her home turf, and show her that I wouldn't be pushed around, and that my heart and my body weren't hers to control.

I walked down the quiet hallway to the closed door to our usual lecture hall. On it, I was surprised to find a note taped.

Class is canceled today. Birdie Johnson, please report to my office. Professor Judge

Oh.

I'd never had reason to visit her office, and my knees fairly knocked at the prospect. Squaring off with her in front of an audience didn't seem so terrible, although I supposed she might blurt out something about my having sex with my English professor, who happened to be her husband, an accusation that had the potential, with no supporting evidence, to send my life and Cary's spiraling out of control.

As I climbed the stairs to the second floor, I wondered what sort of trap awaited me. Would she have the dean with her? Campus security?

On the third step, my feet stopped and refused to keep climbing.

My phone buzzed, and I glanced down to see a text message from Kai.

I can't decide what would smell better, you or a field of tulips, daffodils, and hyacinths. I'm thinking you. I'm thinking about you. You're the prettiest flower in the entire field.

I couldn't help but smile, and suddenly my feet were moving again.

The office with 'Joan Judge' on the frosted glass was the third on the right.

"Come in," she called when I knocked.

I walked in, prepared for the worst.

"Hello, Birdie," she said as I came through the door.

"Should I sit?" I asked, my hand on the arm of a chair opposite her desk.

"No, this will only take a moment, no need to sit down, dear."

Not what I was expecting.

"First of all, I'd like to apologize for the other day. I was out of line."

I arched an eyebrow and tilted my head in confusion.

"I'd like to forget the whole thing," she continued.

"I don't understand," I replied. "What exactly does that mean?"

"It means—live and let live. What you do, who you choose to sleep with, is none of my business."

What the fucking fuck?

She returned to whatever she was working on before I came in.

"That's it?" I said after being ignored for a few moments.

"Unless you have a question about class?" she said,

looking up from her work. When I said nothing, she went back to what she was doing.

I shrugged and left the way I'd come in, baffled by the exchange.

How on earth had Cary ever been married to that woman?

I was relieved that my scholarship, academic standing, and place in the university seemed secure, and that Cary's career was unthreatened, but what had just transpired made very little sense.

On the way back to the dorm, I spotted Jessa working the coffee cart, so I stopped for a visit.

I explained what happened with Professor Judge, and she laughed.

"Blake must be one hell of a persuasive guy," she said. "He managed to get your clothes off and to get his wife to be totally okay with it."

"Ex-wife," I corrected.

"Fair enough. So, what's next? In your love life, I mean?"

"That's the big mystery, right?" I answered. "It's not like I can date all three of them at once, and as much as I loved hooking up with them, no guy is going to be into sharing."

"Didn't you tell me that TA dude went down on you after Professor Vale, you know…"

I blushed. "Yeah. He did."

"I don't see how it would work, but it sounds to me like at least two of them are into having you at the same time. I bet you can figure out where to put a third dick if it comes to that. Just have fun, girl!"

"You're crazy," I insisted.

"*Jealous* is what I am," she said. "If you can't handle the three of them, send one my way. I am so over Wellshire guys. I'm ready to go on the Birdie Johnson plan. I think Roxy is, too."

"Well, there are a lot of professors on campus," I joked. "Happy hunting."

"Maybe I need to switch majors. My professors are not exactly fuckable."

"There'll be a new batch next year. There are always new faces on the faculty. And you're hot," I said.

"And I have free coffee!"

"Bingo!"

We hugged goodbye, and I continued back to the dorm. But I'd only made it a few steps when my phone buzzed with a text from Cary.

Do you have time to come by my place?

On my way, I replied.

I ran-walked to Cary's house, so eager I was to see him and find out what he wanted. And when I arrived I was doubly—or should I say triply?—thrilled to find him joined by Kai and Leo, all in T-shirts and jeans, having just helped to set up a new dining table with four chairs.

I dropped my backpack by the door and kicked off my sneakers. "Hey, guys."

"How did everything go with Professor Judge?" Kai asked.

"It was so odd," I explained. "She basically said 'let bygones be bygones, forget the whole thing'. She completely reversed course. As if someone had called her off."

I looked at the guys expectantly. They had to be behind her change of heart. Assuming she had a heart.

Cary leaned back and smiled.

Leo's and Kai's eyes were wide.

"How the hell did you pull that off, Cary?" Leo asked.

"Simple. I told her that I knew about her affair with the president of the university. While we were married."

Every mouth in the room hung open except Cary's.

"Get serious," Leo insisted.

"I am serious," Cary said. "I found out about it around three years ago. She never knew that I knew."

"The accusations about your sleeping with students make sense now," Kai said.

"Oh yeah." Cary nodded. "Throw anything and everything at the wall and hope something sticks. That way, I'm the bad guy, and if her dirty deeds are discovered, she can point the finger at her awful husband and say he drove her into another man's arms. And bed."

"He has always struck me as slimy," I said. "The president, I mean."

"He cheats at golf, I can testify to that," Leo said, and we all laughed.

"I wish I could have seen the look on her face when you mentioned the affair," Kai added.

"Oh, it was classic," Cary said. "Pure shock and terror. If it ever got out that she'd slept with him, they'd both be in for a world of hurt. To think she threatened me with the same. Such a hypocrite. So, she backed right off. And signed the divorce papers, too."

I smiled so hard it hurt. "So, you're officially unmarried now?"

"I am," he said, joining me on the ottoman. "And I'm sorry about this whole business with her, and me not being technically divorced. It wasn't fair to you."

I hugged his neck, and he wrapped his arms around me in a warm embrace. He released me and held just my hands, turning to face me.

"Before you arrived, we were talking about you, Birdie. And us. And we've reached a decision, something we'd like to run by you."

Butterflies flickered in my stomach as I glanced around the room at everyone.

"Yes?" I asked.

In unison, all three men stood and began removing their clothes. I swallowed hard and everything between my legs began to tingle.

23

PROFESSOR CARY BLAKE

BY THE TIME I was undressed, my cock was already hard. I wasted no time kneeling in front of Birdie and kissing her. Kai was to my right, Leo to my left. They approached on each side, and in my peripheral vision I could see that the situation had brought them to full attention as well.

Birdie broke away just long enough to pull off her top and bra and toss them aside, followed by her yoga pants. She wore no panties.

I took her hand and we ran up the stairs to the bedroom like excited little kids, with Kai and Leo right behind us, laughing.

I lay her down in the center of the bed on her back, and the three of us were instantly upon her. Kai bent to kiss her mouth, Leo her breasts, and I began at her thighs. Six hands explored her body, and she writhed under our ministrations.

As if we were rotating, Leo's lips found Birdie's after mine, and Kai turned his attention to her breasts. She groaned into Leo's open mouth as Kai dragged his knuckles across her taut nipples. I noticed her hands seeking out their dicks, and she started stroking when she found them.

Birdie's thighs fell open, glistening. I needed no further invitation, and I crawled up toward her pussy until I could smell her sweet scent.

The fragrance was intoxicating, and I dove in for all I was worth. My mouth surrounded everything she had to offer, kissing and sucking as my tongue explored. Her back arched up off the bed, and I heard her make a muffled 'mmm' sound as Leo positioned himself next to her and she accepted his cock into her mouth.

I circled her clit with my tongue, giving it the occasional flick and eliciting a garbled whimper each time.

When she seemed close to climax, I moved away, licking my lips. All I wanted from life was to keep eating her pussy, but I wanted to give Kai a chance at her treasure.

He slipped on a condom and replaced me between her legs, up on his knees, easing his fat cock into her.

She was moaning while Leo fucked her face. I lay next to her, taking it all in.

"You're so beautiful, Birdie," I said into her ear. She released Leo's cock and rolled her face to kiss me.

Her face was wild with lust, flushed pink with droplets of sweat dotting her forehead.

Kai was fucking her in earnest now, my headboard building up a steady 'Thump! Thump! Thump!' from his efforts.

"Come now. Come all over Kai's big dick," I told her. "It's so hot watching you get fucked."

"Am I a good girl?" she managed to whimper just before her first climax overtook her.

"Such a good girl," Leo said from the other side of her.

"Watch me," she pleaded. "Watch me come so fucking hard!"

True to her word, she shook and thrashed on the bed, howling as Kai ramrodded her with his cock.

As she came down, Leo leaned in close and said, "My turn, pretty girl." He lay next to her with his rigid cock pointed skyward.

Kai withdrew, slick with her fluids and Leo helped her roll over on top of him as he scooted into the center of the bed.

She sank down slowly and shuddered. Her head hung between her shoulders as her hips began rolling in circles and rocking on Leo's dick. He reached for her, pulling her down onto his chest, a hand on the small of her back to press her down against him.

"Did you fuck her ass?" Kai asked as we watched her riding our colleague.

"No," I replied to my TA. "But she has a great one, doesn't she?"

I nodded and gave my hard-on a tug. I wasn't sure

she was ready for a dick back there yet, but I thought something else might be fun.

I crawled down between Leo's spread legs and put my hands on Birdie's immaculate behind. I helped her along on her ride, spreading her cheeks each time she descended Leo's full length.

She buried her face in Leo's neck as she came, and I watched her most private parts respond. I leaned in and gave her backside a long, slow lick.

She turned back toward me, eyes wide, and I repeated the motion. "Oh fuck, that's so filthy," she hissed, and started ride Leo faster. My tongue was flattened in her ass, swiping up and down as she bounced.

The pitch of her moans and shrieks increased as I zeroed in on her core, plunging inside. "Oh, fuck! Fuck!" she screamed.

Leo roared as he emptied himself, and by the time they both came down from their respective climaxes, they were spent. Birdie rolled off, and Leo looked like he was in shock.

"I have never come that hard in my life," he announced.

Birdie was on her back, hands resting on her body as she tried to process her short-circuiting nerve endings.

Kai climbed on top of her, supporting himself on his elbows and knees, kissing her back to a state of semi-lucidity. He slid his wide dick into her, and I watched her toes flex in response.

His first few thrusts were slow and careful, but he rapidly picked up speed.

"Yes, yes, yes," she chanted, a mantra that continued and got louder as he fucked her harder.

"You feel so fucking good, Birdie," Kai growled, and she held on for dear life as yet another orgasm crashed into her. She clutched at Kai with both hands, her 'yes, yes, yes' turning into one long 'Fuuuuccccckkkk!" as she exploded in sheer ecstasy.

"I need you, Cary," she managed to whisper. "I need to taste your cock."

My dick throbbed at her wicked proclamation, and Kai withdrew long enough for Birdie to roll over onto all fours. I sat at the head of the bed, my erection twitching and leaking everywhere.

Kai entered her from behind and she let out a satisfied "Ahhhhh," as she adjusted to the new angle of penetration.

Once she was used to accommodating his girth in that new way, she lowered her face and for the first time, I felt those wondrous lips on my aching cock.

She focused on the sensitive head, circling it with her tongue as passionately as I was used to her doing to my mouth.

I let my head fall back and focused everything on my dick, wishing I could shut down four of my senses and devote everything I had to touch, to enjoying her mouth on me to the absolute fullest.

Kai grunted with the effort of fucking Birdie harder

and harder, yet never once did her teeth graze my sensitive flesh—it was all lips and tongue.

Without warning, my climax shot through the end of my dick, surprising both of us. I felt like an inexperienced college guy again, losing all control under Birdie's attention. She grinned as I finished, licking my shaft with long, slow strokes, until I had to ease away from the overwhelming sensation.

It was all Kai and Birdie now, and he had set up a hard, fast rhythm, the sounds of their bodies slapping together and echoing off my bedroom walls.

"You're f-fucking me s-so fucking h-hard," Birdie groaned as Leo and I ran our hands all over her body.

I reached beneath her and found her clit, forming a V with my fingers and trapping it in the crux of them.

She collapsed when they finished, completely drained, and Leo curled in behind her, stroking her hair and kissing her shoulders. She wrapped a leg across me and nestled against my chest. Kai wound up sideways across the bottom of the bed, kissing and rubbing her feet.

As the four of us lay there, tangled, exhausted, drenched in sweat and other bodily fluids, I rose to one elbow, looking down at Birdie's beautiful face. Her smile was one of complete contentment and pure bliss, and I was thrilled at having helped her there.

"Is there any chance, and I know how odd this sounds, but is there any chance you'd be interested in dating—*all* of us?" I asked. "This is what I started bringing up before... well, before we got sidetracked and ended up in bed."

She laughed, a sweet laugh of pure joy. "I thought you'd never ask!"

EPILOGUE

My unique relationship, the one where I dated three handsome, amazing men all at once, falling in love with each of them separately and together, was growing in its intensity every day.

It was mid-summer, and the four of us were camping out in the rustic lake house Leo had bought years ago with his earnings from Three Seasons in Scarsdale.

We spent our days in or near the water, and night usually meant I'd be getting fucked senseless by three men who wanted nothing more than to make me have so many orgasms all three of us lost count.

One afternoon, as Cary and Kai sat on the dock trying to catch dinner, I gave Leo a long, slow blowjob on the back deck overlooking the lake.

I knelt there, making love to his big dick with my mouth, taking my time bringing him right to the edge again before backing off. He was a trembling, moaning mess, completely at my mercy.

Just the way I liked him.

His phone buzzed on the side table, and he ignored it until I stopped sucking him long enough to suggest that he answer. I wanted to see how well he could carry on a conversation while I serviced him.

"Hello," he croaked.

I increased the pace and depth of my sucking, and he tensed, urgently gripping a handful of my curls. "Yes, this is Leo Vale," he said in a shaky voice.

"Are you serious," he continued, bolting upright. "Next week? Absolutely. No, I don't currently, but I'll arrange something. Yes. Sure."

He threw a sexy wink my way.

"Thank you so much for calling. Excellent. Yes. Email the proposal so I can look it over. Yes, that address is fine. Thanks again."

After he hung up, I took his cock in my hands and stroked it as he spoke.

"Evidently, some influencer with zillions of Instagram followers is a fan of my old book Three Seasons in Scarsdale, *and she wrote a long post about it with a picture of the cover. It's experienced some kind of resurgence. It's done so well, in fact, that I've been offered a deal to turn it into a screenplay."*

I inhaled his cock, this time wasting no time bringing him off. He came in my mouth, and I swallowed it like a good girl.

"That's incredible," I said, jumping up and into his arms.

"I know you love that book," he recalled.

"I do," I said.

"How would you like to help me with the screenplay?" Leo offered.

"Me?"

"You're a gifted writer, Birdie," he said. "With your help cleaning it up, it would be a smash!"

"I'd be honored," I said.

Kai and Cary were equally excited for their friend, and over the remains of that summer, the four of us pitched in to turn the novel into something that might someday appear in on the big screen.

I say might, because you never know with these movie things.

Summer wrapped and we reluctantly closed down the lake house for the winter, but not before musing about someday, maybe, calling it home on a full-time basis. But that was a long way into the future.

The good news was that Leo was able to negotiate a sabbatical to work on a sequel to Three Seasons in Scarsdale into the next semester. It was exactly what he needed to get past the burnout that had been plaguing him.

Just as awesome, Kai was slotted into a new position in the English department and was on his way to professorship. He found his love of teaching had nothing to do with his family legacy. He and the profession were a perfect match for each other regardless of the work of his late father and grandfather. He still wore tattered jeans and flip flops year-round, but that didn't stop him from being named as 'the newest hot teacher at Wellshire.' Of course, it didn't hurt that he was a cuter version of Prince Harry with his red hair and big smile.

Cary had begun making noises about expanding our little foursome into even more of a family thing. Yeah, after all his years of avoiding children with the woman who was now his ex-wife, he'd started making noises about having babies. With me. Talk about being floored.

I explained to him that while I was beyond honored, I had college to finish, and would like to get a few years of career under my belt before I could really consider such a thing. He swept me into his arms for being open to the idea and assured me that neither he, nor the other guys, were going anywhere. We had plenty of time to create whatever sort of family we wanted.

But I knew the appeal of fatherhood was never far from his thoughts. I could see it in his eyes. It was one of the things I loved about him.

I kept my shared dorm room with Jessa, although I hardly ever slept there, having moved pretty much all my things out. Roxy crashed there all the time, at least when she wasn't cleaning rooms at the hotel, and Jessa was glad for the company.

But I could see she wanted more. She wanted something along the lines of what I had—love and commitment. She'd been there for me, encouraging me to try new and... different things. Look where it got me.

Now it was my turn to help her. Or, at least encourage her. And I don't mean by telling her to write an embarrassing essay for English class.

Jessa liked where I'd ended up so much that she'd been talking about finding her own professor. Or professors. As beautiful and accomplished as she was, I knew she'd have no problem finding someone worthy of all she had to offer. She knew she had my support. In fact, there was an art teacher she'd been talking about an awful lot lately...

So, none of us knew exactly how things in the future would roll out, but we all had each other. And that was more than enough.

BONUS EXTENDED EPILOGUE...

What happens next with Birdie and her three
hot men?
Check out this BONUS Extended Epilogue

I hope you loved reading this book as much as I loved writing it. Please visit my store to learn more about my books, and to buy directly from me! https://mikalaneshop.com/

Dear Reader:

I'm USA TODAY bestselling romance author Mika Lane, and am OBSESSED with bringing you sassy, steamy stories with imperfect heroines and the bad-a*s dudes they bring to their knees. I'll always bring you my signature humor and heat, topped off with a modern-day happily ever after.

My first book ever was *The Day I Ate the Milkyway*, a true fourth-grade masterpiece illustrated with crayons and bound with construction paper and glue. Nowadays, steamy romance gives purpose to my days and nights as I create worlds and characters that tickle the imagination. I live in magical Northern California with my own handsome alpha dude, sometimes known as Mr. Mika Lane, and two devilish cats named Chuck and Murray.

A dual citizen of the United States and Ireland, I have on more than one occasion spent my last dollar on a plane ticket somewhere, and am always planning my next escape. I often try new recipes on unsuspecting friends, search out hiding places to read undisturbed, and sadly kill every houseplant I bring home.

I LOVE to hear from readers when I'm not dreaming up naughty tales to share. Visit my online shop https://mikalaneshop.com/ and say hello https://mikalaneshop.com/pages/meet-mika.

xoxo, Mika